I0451759

DEATH

IS LAGER THAN

LIFE

THE POSSUMWOOD MYSTERIES BOOK 10

HOLLY DEY

Death is Lager Than Life: The Possumwood Mysteries Book 10 © 2022 by Holly Dey. All rights reserved.

Black Mare Books

First Edition 2022

No part of this publication may be reproduced, stored in or introduced into a retrieval system, or transmitted, in any form, or by any means (electronic, mechanical, photocopying, recording, or otherwise) without the prior written permission of both the copyright owner and the above publisher of this book, except for brief quotations in articles and reviews.

This is a work of fiction. Names, characters, places, brands, media, and incidents are either the product of the author's imagination or are used fictitiously. The author acknowledges the trademarked status and trademark owners of various products referenced in this work of fiction, which have been used without permission. The publication/use of these trademarks is not authorized, associated with, or sponsored by the trademark owners.

ISBN: 978-1-959008-15-6

Photo credits:
Jack-o'-lantern: Adobe Stock
Beer mug: Adobe Stock

Acknowledgements

I couldn't do this without the love and support of my wonderful family. I love you so much!

Chapter 1

PRIMROSE CORVINA DONOVAN, better known as PC, came in from feeding her mama's rescue critters and set the wire basket of blue, green, and brown eggs on the counter. As she washed her hands in the kitchen sink, her smallish terrier mix, Cordite, waited impatiently for a piece of chicken jerky.

"Oh, my goodness!" Rose Donovan stared wide-eyed at this morning's edition of the *Possumwood Press*, the local paper.

"What is it, Mama?"

"I can't believe it! I know Velma Rogers. Or at least I thought I did. She seemed so nice."

Trying not to trip over the dancing dog, PC moved to look over her shoulder.

The front-page headline blared, "Woman Lives With Rotting Corpse in Social Security Scam" in forty-eight point type. A picture of a disheveled elderly woman being led away in handcuffs took up most of the rest of the page.

Wouldn't be the first time. Twenty-five years as a homicide detective had made PC… a little jaded.

The detective shrugged. "Did she kill him? Or just fail to report his death? Perhaps his Social Security was their only income."

Rose snapped the paper down. "That's still fraud!"

PC raised her hands. "I'm not defending her. I'm just saying that the prospect of starvation tends to change peoples' values."

Rose considered the front page for a moment, then opened the paper to read the rest of the story.

Cordite capered around the kitchen, and PC opened a cabinet and retrieved a treat for him. She made him work for it, and the more tricks he did, the more excited he got, running through every skill he knew, except for the one she asked for.

"You're hopeless." She gave him the treat, and he ran into the living room to eat it.

"Oh, my! Poor Norville. It says here that his mummified remains were found in a back bedroom, wrapped in newspaper and blankets. How awful."

"Who discovered the body?"

"The po-lice. But it was all due to the investigative reportin' of Bradford Penney. He bought the *Possumwood Press* a couple of months ago. Seems like he's takin' it in a new direction. Says here he's been workin' on '…an exposé that will shake Possumwood to its core.' What do you think he's talkin' about?"

PC shrugged. "Your guess is as good as mine. Is Possumwood ready for the next generation of muckrakers?"

Rose raised an eyebrow and returned to her newspaper.

"Hey, Mama. Has Rocky already left for work?"

"I believe he has, honey."

The detective's brother worked as a certified nursing assistant at Azalea Manor, the local nursing home. He was trying to get his life together after decades of alcohol addiction. She just wanted to know if he was interested in going out for dinner tonight, though.

"I'll text him later. Where are you and Terry going this evening to celebrate?"

"Not sure. He said it was a surprise."

When she'd come back to her hometown to take care of Rose after she'd fallen and broken her hip, PC had struggled with the prospect of her mother having a boyfriend. The detective had really warmed to Terry since she arrived. Rose had been alone for a long time after her husband's murder, and Terry was good for her. Their first official date had been going on one of the *Happily Ever Afters* bed-and-breakfast/wedding venue's Halloween ghost tours, so they considered October third their anniversary.

The Afters ran the tours every weekend in October, leading up to their Halloween Ball extravaganza on the last Saturday of the month. But first, there was Oktoberfest at the *Biersal Brew Pub*, Possumwood's craft brewery. She was glad the festivities started on a Friday (today), because she met up with friends there every Wednesday night to play darts and socialize. Big events upset the laid-back ambiance.

The Biersal was hosting a lunchtime sausage and beer celebration dubbed *The Best Wurst Fest*. Drew Burlesconi had talked her into going with him. There would even be a live oompah band in the biergarten. How could she say no to that?

Drew owned *The Best Little Art Gallery in Texas*, and was probably her closest friend in Possumwood, even though she'd grown up there, and she'd only met him a few months ago.

It didn't hurt that he was a good-looking man, and he seemed to know at least something about everything, and his knowledge of art was encyclopedic. He held Saturday art workshops at his gallery, and he'd encouraged her to enter the county fair art show last month. Still amazed she'd won second place. More than anything else, though, he made her laugh. And that was something she hadn't realized how much she'd needed.

"Did you say you were goin' to the sausage party with Drew for lunch?" Rose folded up her paper.

PC chuckled. "The what? You mean the *Best Wurst Fest*? Yes. I'm meeting him there in about half an hour."

Parking was going to be terrible. PC typically walked or jogged to the Biersal for Wednesday night darts anyway—it was only a mile or so from Rose's house—so that was her plan. Drew lived even closer to it than she did.

When she arrived, the *Brisk Rib Barbecue* had several smoker trailers set up in the parking lot. PC wasn't overly fond of sausage but proceeds from the lunch plate sales benefitted the local Lions' Club, and she was happy enough to support them.

Drew waved to her from the ticket booth, and she changed course to meet him. They bought their lunch tickets and stepped over to the tables to make their selections.

An odd thumping noise came from their left. PC looked around but didn't see anything unusual.

Bratwurst, bockwurst, knockwurst, and leberkäse were all standard sausage-colored offerings, but there were also yellow gelbwurst, white weisswurst, and black blutwurst.

The thumping came again. "Did you hear that?"

"Hear what?" Drew asked.

"Kind of a sputtering, knocking. Like a car running out of gas."

He shook his head.

The sausage plate included a choice of IPA, stout, lager, or the Biersal's famous, or infamous, depending on who was doing the talking, persimmon ale.

Drew picked up a can with a bright orange persimmon on it. "You finally going to try it?"

"When pigs fly."

There was a thump. Then a whoosh.

One of the barbecue trailers exploded and lunch-goers yelped and ducked for cover.

Flaming sausages shot into the sky, only to blow apart like fatty fireworks. A couple of them erupted directly over Drew and PC, splattering them with grease, meat, and spices.

Fortunately, no one had been standing close to the grill when it went up. Frank Smith, the trailer's owner, quickly doused it with a fire extinguisher.

Drew licked some sausage juice from his upper lip and offered the can of persimmon ale to PC again. "How about now?"

"I don't think so."

They cleaned up as best they could in the Biersal's restrooms, but they had both lost their appetite for sausage.

Drew picked PC up for the Saturday night Oktoberfest event. They parked at his house and walked the three blocks over to the brew pub. When they got to the entrance and saw how many people were packed inside, the detective almost changed her mind about attending. Drew held the door, and she reluctantly shuffled inside.

PC felt like every one of the roughly ten thousand people who called Possumwood home were crammed into the Biersal. She disliked crowds—they made her feel depleted, as if the crush of bodies was leaching away her life force. The river of people flowed toward the back of the building, where the brewery was housed.

The first tour of the facility was about to start. There would be several throughout the evening. The base notes of the oompah band tuba outside in the biergarten vibrated through her body. The bar and dining area of the Biersal Brew Pub was cavernous but felt close with the crush of humanity. Perhaps once the tour was over, they'd go outside and get some air.

She was cheered to see a familiar face. "Dr. Mack!" She waved, and he responded, but the crowd was too thick for them to easily move toward each other.

The Medical Examiner was holding the hand of an elegant, silver-haired woman, whom PC assumed to be his wife.

Stan Zimmerman, one of the twins who owned the Biersal, stood on a wooden crate near a steel door. "Please make sure you stay behind the railing and please, please, please don't touch anything. When I open the door, the first thing we'll see is the malter, where barley is prepared to make beer."

"Just like a winery, the best part of the tour is the tasting at the end," Drew nudged PC.

Zimmerman continued. "We soak it in water to start the germination process, and then we toss it in the roaster to dry out. Next, we mash, or soak, the malted barley and drain off the excess liquid. What's left is called the wort. That goes in the boiler with hops and other flavorings."

"I'm curious about what flavorings they put in there. Especially that persimmon ale," PC said quietly.

"After that's cooked, we add yeast and sometimes more hops, then transfer the liquid into open fermentation vats. After that, closed vats to finish. Then two to three weeks later, depending on what we're making, we bottle and enjoy."

With a flourish, he opened the door and beer tourists filed through into the chamber of mysteries. Stainless steel equipment stood on all sides of the room, segmented into groups by a metal railing. The brew peepers shuffled down a wide path between the sections. The brewmeister walked backwards, pointing out burlap bags of barley and plastic bags of pelleted hops. PC wondered if it was possible to get drunk just from the smell of the brewing ale. The hops were almost overpowering.

Zimmerman tapped on the railing to get everyone's attention. "All right. We started our special Oktoberfest brew three weeks ago. It's ready to bottle, and you will be the first to taste it!"

As the walkway came to a T-intersection and the crowd filled in, a scream stopped the discourse on lautering.

The brewer turned around, then ducked between the bars of the railing and ran toward one of the large square tanks.

A pair of legs, dressed in brown slacks, hung out of the fermenting tank closest to the railing.

Chapter 2

"Stan! Get everyone out of here. I'll call the PD." PC fumbled for her phone. Panic rippled over the crowd, and people began shouting and struggling against each other. "Stan! Now!"

The detective hurried to the dangling legs, hoping it wasn't too late. But the appendages were stiff as stone. He'd been like that for at least a couple of hours.

Zimmerman stumbled onto the pathway. "Calm down!"

Even PC, who was a dozen feet away, barely heard him above the uproar. Two loud clangs of metal on metal silenced the noise.

Drew had found a short length of pipe and banged it against the railing. "People! Please make an orderly exit back the way you came."

Since he was the one who headed off the stampede, Drew helped Stan herd the would-be beer tasters out of the brewing area. Now that she could hear, PC put a call in to the Possumwood PD.

She hung up with Annie, the dispatcher, as the Medical Examiner approached with his companion.

"Now, I was not expecting a call during Oktoberfest." Dr. Mack—short for McKenzie Chapman—shook his head. "PC, have you met my beautiful bride, Arabella?"

"Nice to meet you, Mrs. Chapman." She cut her eyes to the forlorn legs hanging from the edge of the fermenter.

"Dr. Chapman, actually." Arabella started toward the corpse. "I'm also a pathologist, although *I'm* not retired." She glanced over her shoulder at her spouse. "I've assisted my husband on a number of cases, if you're concerned about my being squeamish."

"Dr. Chapman. I'd be honored."

Dr. Mack and PC fell into line behind her, and they stopped at the railing in front of the vat. Foam bubbled around the decedent's waist, which disappeared beneath the thick layer of froth.

PC snapped a few pictures while they waited on Possumwood's finest. Six rectangular vats sat on risers off the concrete floor. The containers themselves were roughly five feet tall, but a little wider and longer. She pulled out her notebook and made a quick sketch.

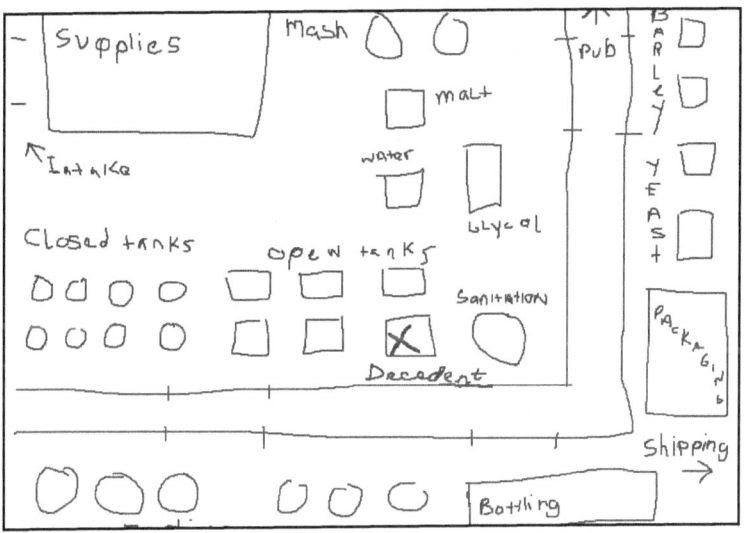

"I'll need to go get my equipment," Dr. Mack said. "Shouldn't take long—we're only a few blocks from the funeral home." He gave his wife a peck on the cheek and headed toward the exit.

Police Chief Elwood "Woody" Wilson and Officers Tran and Gorman intercepted the ME. After speaking with him for a moment, he continued out, and they marched toward PC and Arabella.

Woody shook his head. "Donovan. Why am I not surprised?"

"Because I called it in?"

"That, too."

PC turned to her friend. "Hey, Tran. I see you drew the short straw on duty roster, huh?"

His lips curled upward. "It's okay. I'm taking two weeks off for my honeymoon next month."

"Where are you and Annie going?"

"Jamaica—Montego Bay."

"I'm sure you'll have a great time. Have you been there before?"

"I haven't. Annie has when she was a little kid, though."

"Hey, Tran!" Woody called from where he stood near the rigid legs. "Were you going to help pull this guy out, or is this a social call?"

Gorman was nearby, holding his cellphone in his hand.

Tran hurried over to the vat.

"Wait!" PC, followed by Arabella, was close behind Tran. "Don't you want to photograph the scene?"

Woody gestured to the older officer. "That's what Gorman's been doing while y'all were over there flappin' your gums."

A glint of green light a short distance from the vat caught PC's eye. "What's this?"

Arabella squatted by the railing to get a closer look. "It's a sword."

"A what?" PC asked.

"One of those little plastic swords that come in cocktails with a cherry or olive."

The detective took her own snap before Gorman got set up. He shot her a scowl, and she replied with a smile.

A few more photographs later, Woody asked. "You ready?"

Gorman nodded and put his phone away. The Possumwood Police Department didn't have the budget for a crime scene photographer, so on rare occasions when it was required, officers took their own pictures, usually with their cell phones.

Woody was the tallest, so he reached into the foam for a shoulder, while Gorman and Tran wrangled the rigid legs.

"Ah! Perfect timing." Dr. Mack returned with a plastic tackle box of medical equipment.

Arabella raised her hand. "Wait! Is there a tarp or something we can put him on?"

Tran looked around and found some plastic sheeting. The doctor used his scalpel to cut it, and they worked together to arrange it at the foot of the fermenter.

The decedent was in the throes of rigor mortis, so Gorman stood and reached into the tank for the other shoulder. They pulled the dead man out, his body bent almost exactly in half, and laid him on the plastic-covered concrete floor.

Arabella gasped. "Isn't that Bradford Penney?"

It took a moment for PC to realize who that was. "The newspaper guy? What was he doing in here?"

Tran searched the man's pockets. "Maybe he found out what's really in persimmon ale, and they had to kill him."

Woody cleared his throat.

Dr. Mack took the corpse's temperature, then looked at his watch and wrote it down.

"Based on the progression of the rigor, I'm going to say he likely died between 8 AM and 4 PM, give or take a little. The temperature of the lager in the tank is 58°, according to this thermometer—he gestured to a cluster of dials and gauges at the front of the tank—so that would have both slowed down the onset and cooled his body faster, so it's tricky to estimate. There is a laceration behind his left ear. Might be blunt force trauma, but I'll have to get him on the table to confirm."

The ME went back to collecting evidence. "Hey, Gorman! Can you help me with his fingerprints?"

Gorman shuffled over to assist.

A shaken Stan Zimmerman returned to the crime scene. His mouth opened a little when he caught sight of the decedent. "Brad?" he queried the corpse.

Woody and Tran pulled him aside, away from the dead man. PC moved so that she could hear the interview.

"Do you mind if I record our conversation, Mr. Zimmerman?" the young officer asked.

"It's… fine. I guess."

Woody gave a slight nod. "Stan? Do you know who that is over there?"

"Yeah. Brad Penney. He's new in town. Owns the paper. He was doing a story about our brewery. He'd mostly been talking to Ken, so I can't tell you much about it, although he might have given Brad a tour when he came in this morning to check the fermenters."

"Any idea what time?"

"My brother usually gets here between 7:30 and 8:00. No idea what time he would have been meeting Brad, or if that was even scheduled for today."

Tran's radio crackled and chirped. "Zebra-230, do you copy? What is your 10-20?"

He paused the recording. "Dispatch, I'm 10-6."

"10-4, Zebra-230. When you are 10-26, see Simone Reynolds at the Afters to 10-63 a burglary."

"10-4. Copy that, Dispatch." Tran restarted the recording. "Sorry."

Woody rubbed his temple. "Where were we? Have you spoken with Ken today?"

"No. Marlene, Keryn, and I were in the front of the house, getting it set up for the event this evening. He was handling the back. I've been crazy busy all day and haven't seen him."

"And how is Marlene?"

Stan blinked a few times. "My wife is fine."

"You think Keryn will know where Ken is? She is his wife, after all."

"I have no idea. She's in the kitchen, baking pretzels, if you want to ask her. He may even be in there helping her."

Woody gave a gentle nod. "We'll talk to her in a few minutes. Now, you didn't think it was unusual that you hadn't seen Ken all day?"

"I had my hands full and I didn't really notice, but now that I think about it, yeah, it is strange. I mean, I assume he's here somewhere. I just haven't seen him."

"Why don't you give him a call and ask him to come back here?"

Stan nodded. "Sure." He pulled out his phone, tapped the screen, and held it up to his ear.

The theme song from *2001: A Space Odyssey*, "Thus Spake Zarathustra," began to play faintly.

Stan's ears pricked up, and he followed the sound. Tran and Woody shadowed him. PC trailed surreptitiously behind them.

The music was coming from behind the glycol cooling unit. A few tools were scattered on top of a rumpled burlap bag. Ominous kettle drums pounded from underneath the equipment.

The percussion fell silent in mid-beat.

Stan slowly lowered his device. "That's Ken's phone."

Chapter 3

STAN ZIMMERMAN REACHED for his brother's cell phone.

"Wait!" Tran grabbed his arm. "Sorry, but that's evidence."

"Evidence of what?"

Woody put a hand on Stan's shoulder. "I don't want to alarm you. But Mr. Penney's killer may have taken Ken with him."

Or Ken may be the killer and left his phone behind so he couldn't be tracked.

PC liked to think she knew the Zimmerman brothers reasonably well, and that Ken would never do anything like that. Prisons were filled with people who would never have done anything like that, though.

The glycol unit rattled and groaned. Stan applied some percussive maintenance and adjusted a few dials. "We've been having trouble with this thing all week."

Perhaps the killer hadn't noticed Ken working on it until after the deed was done. That would be a real problem for Ken. Is that why the tools were scattered around and the phone was left behind, under the machinery? Ken had left in a hurry.

Was he hiding from the killer?

Taken by the killer?

Or was he the killer?

In addition to the exit to the pub, there was a loading dock for finished product and a smaller door on the opposite side where supplies, like barley, were brought in. She supposed Ken might have crept behind equipment and exited the supply door, but if that had happened, where was he now?

His absence suggested a sinister situation.

Woody chewed the inside of his cheek. "Tran, Bourgeois, and Sanchez are on the way. Why don't you go run that 10-26, since it's just across the street? Then go back to the station and file your reports. Thanks for filling in."

"Sure thing."

Woody headed back toward the late Mr. Penney.

Tran passed very close to PC. "Come with me."

"What?"

"I need to talk to you."

PC pointed to the smaller door. "Hey, Woody. You might have your people check that door for any signs of Ken Zimmerman." She left through the shipping exit with Tran.

Most folks in town shortened *Happily Ever Afters* to 'the Afters,' and it was located across the street from the Biersal. There was no side entrance, so they had to walk down Main Street to get to the front gate.

After they were well out of earshot of the other investigators, PC asked, "What did you want to talk about?"

He looked around, as if he were about to divulge a grave secret. "It's Annie."

"What about her?"

"I think… I think she may have changed her mind."

"About marrying you? Why do you say that?"

He sighed and bit his lip. "Well… she seems distant and distracted. When I ask her out to do stuff, she's suddenly too tired, or too busy. I feel like she doesn't want to be around me. At all. Is she trying to tell me something?"

They hurried across Crockett Street. "How much of the wedding planning are you doing?"

"Me? Um... not much. Actually, not really... any."

"Weeeell, people who have never planned a wedding have no idea how much effort it takes. She's working a full-time job, planning the wedding, and the date's getting closer. Her life is about to be very different. It doesn't mean it's bad, or she's changed her mind—even good stress is still stress. Is there anything you can do to take some of the organizing off her shoulders?"

"Well, she and her mom are doing everything, and I'm afraid I'll mess things up if I get involved. I don't want to make an enemy out of my mother-in-law. We get along pretty well right now. Her parents are both Korean. My mom's Japanese and my dad was Vietnamese. So, the ceremony will be mostly American, but with Korean, Japanese, and Vietnamese elements."

"That sound like it's going to be a spectacular event. You can run errands—pick stuff up? Or just cook her dinner and give her a foot rub while you're watching TV."

They paused at the pedestrian entrance next to the locked wrought-iron gates. Tran pushed the buzzer.

"Hello?"

"Simone? It's Hiro. I'm here about your burglary."

"See you in a minute." The lock on the gate buzzed.

Tran and PC walked through. The driveway curved around a pond and a garden with a large Victorian gazebo that matched the house. PC was glad it was night, and the peacocks were asleep. Their alarming cries gave her the creeps. Dim solar lights lined the gravel road at even intervals, alternating sides, but marking the road well enough.

Tran's lips smacked. "You seem to know a lot about wedding planning for someone who's never been married."

"I was three weeks away from getting married."

"Did you get cold feet?"

PC couldn't see the grin on his face but heard it in his voice.

If only... "We got into an argument. Something stupid, like cheesecake versus pie on the dessert menu."

Tran swallowed loudly. "You broke up over that?"

"No. We fought right before Mike left for work. He was killed by a drunk driver while he was working a traffic accident. I didn't get to the hospital in time."

"Oh." Tran was silent for several long moments. "I'm sorry. Really. I shouldn't have been so flippant. That must have been... I can't even imagine."

The driveway continued along the side of the house, leading to guest and restaurant parking, then the exit. They took the flag-stone path to the front door.

Klonk! Klonk! Klonk!

PC's body twitched at each strike of the brass knocker on its shiny metal plate.

Within seconds, Simone Reynolds appeared at the door. "I'm glad you're here. Let me grab a flashlight."

She disappeared inside, then returned with both a flashlight and her wife, Caitlyn, in tow. Tran and PC followed the two women to the side of the house. They passed in front of the extensive vegetable garden to a set of four clotheslines.

Caitlyn tapped one of the metal poles. "I put the bedding out to dry around lunchtime, but I got busy, and forgot about it."

Simone shone her light along the lengths of line. A half dozen bedsheets shrouded the wires. "I came out to get it around eight. All three of the quilts Simone hung out were gone. Sheets were still here. I didn't want to touch anything, so I left them."

Tran and PC examined the empty spaces on the clothesline. There were no footprints in the short, thick grass. No sign that anyone had been there.

The detective turned to the proprietor. "Clothespins? Might be able to get a fingerprint."

Caitlyn shook her head. "They took those, too."

"What time do you lock the gates?" PC asked.

Simone replied. "Unless we're having a public event, like the Valentine's Brunch or the Halloween Ball, they're always locked. The card keys that open the guests' rooms also work on the gates."

"How many guests do you have this weekend?" Tran asked.

"We're at capacity. There are two people in each of the ten guest rooms in the house and the carriage house, which sleeps six, is also full." Simone hugged herself and rubbed her arms.

"But people have been known to climb through the hedge." PC gestured toward the peripheral shrubbery.

Caitlyn nodded. "Of course. I mean, you were here that time those poor girls broke into the garden, looking for food."

Tran wrote in his notepad. "And did you ask your guests if they'd borrowed the quilts?"

Simone nodded. "We asked the ones that were here. Some said they had seen the quilts, but no one admitted to taking them. For the ones who were out, we looked in their rooms, including the coach house. No one had them."

PC tapped her upper lip. "This may seem like it's completely out of left field, but have you been interviewed by or spoken with Bradford Penney at the *Possumwood Press* recently?"

The two women shared a look. Caitlyn's lips pursed. Simone's eyebrows raised.

"*Ugggh.*" Caitlyn groaned. "That insufferable man."

Simone shook her head. "I wish the Press hadn't fallen into his clutches. It's just going to become some tabloid gossip rag. Somebody should do something about him."

Somebody already has. "Really? What did he do to you?"

Caitlyn crossed her arms. "He followed one of our guests through the gate, then when they parked and got out of their car, he started badgering them about their stay. When we came out and asked him to leave, he accused us of inventing the story of Tom Brenderman's ghost for the sake of advertising haunted rooms."

"Said he was going to expose us as frauds!" Simone's hands seemed to take on a life of their own, gesticulating wildly.

"Is that so?" Tran tapped his pen on his notebook. "What were you ladies doing during the day today?"

Simone put a hand on Caitlyn's shoulder. "I left around seven to get some specialty items in Austin. I got back early afternoon. Not sure what time, but the laundry was on the line when I came out to the garden to gather some greens for dinner. The quilts were there."

Caitlyn tilted her chin downward. "I made breakfast for twenty guests from 7:00 – 9:00, then cleaned up the kitchen, loaded the dishwasher, and did housework. Guests have been in and out of the house all day, and I've talked to several of them. Why are you asking? This doesn't seem to have anything to do with our missing quilts."

Tran shifted his weight. "Bradford Penney was found deceased this evening."

Simone and Caitlyn shared a look. Simone ran a hand through her dark hair. "How did he die?"

"Apparently, he drowned."

"How awful."

Caitlyn's eyes narrowed. "Do you think we had something to do with it? I'm not even sure where he lives."

"Oh, he moved into the old Wharton place—"

"Simone!" Caitlyn cut her off.

PC's phone vibrated, and she startled. It was a text from Drew asking where she was. She dashed out a reply. "Afters. Be back in a minute."

Simone and Caitlyn were both about average height and slim to medium build. It was doubtful that one of them could have lifted Penney, who was on the plump side, high enough to force his upper body into the vat. Even working together, it would be a struggle.

Caitlyn crossed her arms. "I'd be willing to bet that half the people in this town had a run-in with Mr. Penney. We were at the library the other day when he marched right up to Abike Sabo and demanded to see her papers. Mildred McClosky kicked him out, but not before he had poor Abike in tears."

Where had PC heard that name before? "Doesn't she work at the vet clinic?"

"Yeah," Tran answered. "My mom loves Abike. She's the only one Kit doesn't bite when Mom takes her to the vet. Fortunately, Kit only weighs, like, six pounds, so she can't really hurt anybody."

Simone took in a sharp breath. "Oh. You know who'd really want Brad dead? Daphne Jones. He all but accused her of murder."

Chapter 4

PC WANTED TO stay and hear more, but guilt about abandoning Drew at the Biersal pricked her. "Tran, do you need anything else from me? I need to get going."

"No, I'm good. Thanks."

"Alright. Hope your quilts turn up, ladies."

The detective walked back to the brew pub. The formerly jubilant crowd was dispersing, and more police vehicles had shown up. Drew was outside, waiting for her.

"So much for Oktoberfest," she said. "What do we do now?"

"You're not going to investigate?"

"I don't have a dog in this fight. If Tran needs me, he'll call."

"Seems like they always need you, sooner or later."

PC took his arm. "My hourly rate is more than fair."

"I suppose we could go to my place. Surely there's something to do there."

"Oh? What did you have in—"

PC's phone rang. "Sorry, I have to take this." She tapped the screen. "Yes, Mama?"

"I hate to bother you, honey. I know you're out on the town and all. But Rocky's workin' a double shift today and Daisy left her medicine at my house. Could you run it out to her?"

"She can drive now. Can't she get it?"

Rose sighed. Loudly. "You do recall she bled half to death? Then had major surgery on top of that. She ain't exactly perky just now."

"I know. Be there soon." PC hung up and turned to Drew. "My sister left some medication at Mama's house. I'm being dispatched to courier it out to her."

"I can drive you."

"I… you don't have to."

"I want to."

"Let's go, then."

They got into Drew's car, and he started it up. "How is Daisy, by the way?"

"I told you we got the pathology report, right? It was just a fibroid. A really huge one, but not cancer. The baby factory had been closed for a while, anyway. They had to give her several units of blood—she's still super anemic, so I can't be too mad at her. She's so pale, she's almost translucent, poor thing."

They retrieved the meds and delivered them to Daisy. She was already in her nightgown and drowsy, so they didn't stay.

As they drove down Justice Avenue toward Drew's house, PC pointed to the back edge of Justice Hardware on their left. "What's going on there? Is someone in the dumpster?"

Drew slowed. "You're right. It looks like… she's stuck."

He pulled into the parking lot of the hardware store, and they got out. A young woman with dark skin and a vibrant yellow and green headscarf was stuck in the small end door of a dumpster. It appeared that the sleeve of her paw-print covered scrubs was caught on something inside.

"You need some help?" PC asked. "What happened?"

"Yes, I don't wish to be out here all night. Thank goodness you showed up!"

PC looked across the street. "You must work at the vet clinic."

"I do. I am Abike Sabo, by the way."

"PC Donovan, and this is my friend, Drew Burlesconi. Everyone speaks so highly of you. I think you've groomed my dog, Cordite."

"A light brown terrier, who is so fond of stinky things?"

"That would be him. You've done an amazing job of decontaminating him a couple of times."

Abike nodded. "Thank you."

Drew opened the lid and shone his phone flashlight inside. PC was grateful the dumpster was filled with lumber scrap and construction waste. She'd dumpster dived in search of evidence a few times before, and it could take a week to get the smell of rotting garbage out of her hair.

Drew pushed the lid open a little further. "I see the problem. You're caught on some bent nails."

Peering around Abike through the small door, PC saw it, too. "You keep holding the light. I think I can get it from here." She moved to the other side of the trapped woman. "I'm going to have to squeeze in front of you and reach my arm inside. I apologize in advance if it gets a little personal."

Abike nodded.

The detective put her hand on Abike's arm and gently groped her way to the impediment. The two nails had caught the fabric of her sleeve like fishhooks, and in her awkward position, PC struggled to free the trapped cloth. After a few tries, she got it loose and both she and Abike stepped away from the dumpster.

"Thank you, thank you! I was throwing some litter away that I picked up off the sidewalk. No good deed goes unpunished, I suppose."

"Glad we could help." Drew smiled and jangled the keys in his pocket. "Can we give you a lift anywhere?"

"I was just walking to my apartment after checking on an HBC patient that came in this afternoon. I do not know how long I have been out here, but long enough to get a chill. I only wish to warm up now."

Drew wrinkled a brow. "HBC?"

"Hit By a Car."

PC glanced at Drew's vehicle. "The truck stop's open, if you want to grab some hot cocoa."

"Perhaps another time. I just want a hot shower."

"Understood. Do you mind if I ask you a couple of quick questions?"

Abike hugged herself. "If they are quick…"

"Of course. I don't want you to get hypothermia. How well did you know Bradford Penney?"

The groomer's face fell from happy to glowering the instant the name 'Bradford' had come out of PC's mouth.

"What is this about?"

"I heard that you had an encounter with him recently, and I wanted to hear your side of the story."

"Are you working for his paper?"

"No. No, of course not."

Abike was silent for several moments. "If you wish to discuss Penney, then I will let you buy me a hot chocolate."

"Deal." PC gave a nod and headed toward Drew's car.

He and Abike followed her, and they were soon on their way to the truck stop.

The groomer stirred whipped cream into her hot cocoa. "Brad Penney was not a good man."

"What makes you say that?" PC asked.

"He was always looking for trouble. One of our clients, Stacey Clemmons—she just won at a major horse show—caught him in the feed room of her barn, searching for performance-enhancing drugs he thought she was giving the horses. He accused me of being here illegally." Abike shook her head.

Drew warmed his hands on his tea mug. "I'm sorry to hear about that."

"My family spent years in a refugee camp in Camaroon. So many people, so few sponsors. Our mother dressed us girls as boys, so we would not be stolen as child brides by Boko Haram. As boys, we got to go to school. That is the best thing I can say about the camp. I came to the US as a teenager, but my parents did everything correctly. I became a citizen as soon as I turned eighteen. I have nothing to hide."

"Probably just trying to increase newspaper circulation. It seems he was bothering a lot of people. I'm sorry you were one of them." The detective sipped her own hot chocolate.

"Why are you asking about Bradford Penney?"

PC rubbed her forehead. "He was found dead this evening."

"And you wish to know who might have wanted him dead?"

"It's common practice to talk to people who knew the victim in an investigation."

"Are you the police?"

"I do some contract work for Possumwood PD from time to time."

"Then I suppose it was lucky for both of us that you found me this evening."

Drew waited while Abike walked through the pedestrian gate at the Persimmon Hill Apartments. Once it locked behind her, he used the turnaround by the gate keypad to get back onto Main Street.

"I thought you weren't investigating." Drew's voice was flat.

"I hadn't planned to. Really. I guess she just fell into my lap. Figuratively speaking. I didn't even think about it. Old habits die hard."

Drew nodded.

PC adjusted her seatbelt. "She didn't ask how he died."

"What?"

"When you tell someone that a person died, usually the first thing they ask is 'How did it happen?' Unless they're well prepared, the killer never asks. They already know. She also referred to him in the past tense."

"Perhaps she was focusing on not celebrating. Besides, she said she'd been at work. That should be easy enough to verify."

"True." PC sucked her teeth. "Would you mind going back to the dumpster where we found Abike?"

"Why?"

"I just want to look for the litter. I'd sleep better tonight if we found it."

"Okay."

He drove to Justice Hardware. PC got out before Drew had even shifted into park. She shone her phone in through the small door. Chunks of wood, jagged slabs of sheetrock, and fragments of tile filled most of the container. Her light glinted off of two empty persimmon ale bottles.

Between them lay a crowbar with red flecks on it.

Chapter 5

DREW'S CAR ROLLED to a stop in Rose's driveway.

"I'm really sorry." PC reached for the door handle. "I'll find a way to make it up to you."

The police response time had been swift, but it had taken a while to give their statements. As time ticked by, hopes of an alternate activity had drained away.

Drew turned and whisked a small piece of debris off of her forehead. "I know. It's who you are."

That almost sounds like a brush off. "What about tomorrow afternoon?"

He shook his head. "I'm working the gallery all afternoon. Maybe dinner?"

"At *Truffles!*" She usually resisted going there, but it *was* Drew's favorite restaurant.

His hand moved from the shifter toward PC.

Light flooded the car as a vehicle pulled up behind them.

PC shielded her eyes. "That must be Rocky. We're in his spot. Goodnight. See you tomorrow."

She got out and shut the door. Rocky backed up to let Drew reverse out. PC watched his taillights disappear around the corner while she waited for her brother to park.

"Hey, Rock."

He yawned. "Not trying to be rude. I pulled a double and I'm tired to the bone. I may not stay awake long enough to get in the house."

"Well… at least it's overtime, right?"

"There's that."

PC pulled open the screen to the front porch. Cordite barked inside. As soon as the door opened, the dog rushed out to dance at PC's feet.

"Rocky, honey? Did you chase Drew away?"

"Mama!" PC shut the door harder than she intended, almost catching Cordite's tail. A well-timed wag was all that kept him from disaster.

"I keep tellin' you, a little romance would do you a world of good."

Rocky raised his hand to about waist height. "Night."

He shuffled to his room.

"Mama…"

"Yes?"

"Nothing. I'm beat. Goodnight."

PC stared at her reflection while she brushed her teeth. Drew was clearly interested in more than friendship. She wasn't opposed to it but wasn't sure it was entirely fair. But then again, lots of people had long-distance relationships. Was that a valid suggestion or merely a rationalization for doing whatever she wanted?

If she returned to Houston in January… If? She'd been so sure before. Couldn't wait to get out of Possumwood when she'd arrived last January. Now, doubt crept in. Just a shadow, but she couldn't deny it was there.

What is that sound?

The pall of sleep resisted her efforts to pull it off. Noise was coming from her right. She reached out a hand and groped around on her nightstand. Her phone was ringing.

"Tran? It's… What time is it?"

"Almost seven. I wanted to give you time to feed your animals before I picked you up."

"Why are you picking me up?"

"We're going to *Bucephalus Sporthorses* to talk to Stacey Clemmons. The only time she was available to meet with us was at 8:00. See you in half an hour." He hung up.

PC yawned. "Nobody has a right to be that cheerful this time of day."

She dressed, fed, brought in the eggs, and even had a bowl of cereal with three minutes to spare before Tran texted that he was outside.

Rocky had Sunday and Monday off. Neither he nor Rose was stirring, so PC crept out of the house, leaving Cordite with a chicken jerky strip to keep him company. For about thirty seconds.

PC got in the squad. "Woody knows Sunday's time and a half, right?"

"I'm sure he does. We still haven't located Ken Zimmerman yet. The Chief's okayed overtime for extra patrols to search for him. Hopefully, it's not a double homicide."

"Or, he could be the killer."

"I hope not. I really hope not. I like the Zimmermans. They've always been very friendly to our family. Either of those two scenarios is terrible."

"Because we're going to see Stacey Clemmons, I'm assuming you spoke with Abike Sabo yesterday."

Tran stopped at a red light. "We did. Found her at the vet clinic, checking on some patients."

"What do you think about her as a suspect?"

"I don't know. She's very fit and strong. Penney... wasn't. Now, did she whack him on the head and put him in the tank? That, I'm not so sure about."

"So, it was blunt force trauma?"

"Yeah. Dr. Mack said the wound was made with a flat, heavy object."

"Like a crowbar?"

"Like a crowbar."

PC steepled her fingers. "Did you get an idea of how scared she might be about being returned to Nigeria? She said she was a refugee."

The light changed, and Tran eased into the intersection. "Not entirely. But I definitely had the impression that she didn't want to go back."

"She's a citizen now, so I don't think they can legally deport her. Unless... she's a convicted felon. But immigration law isn't my wheelhouse."

"You're probably right. I give her a two out of five stars in the possible killer department."

"I agree." PC looked out the window for a moment as the rolling countryside sped past her. "Do you know who Daphne Jones is?"

"Daphne. Jones." Tran repeated the name as if he were tasting it. "Sounds familiar, but I can't think of where I heard it."

"Simone Reynolds said Penney practically accused her of murder."

"Oh! I remember now. She's a hospice nurse."

PC's brow furrowed. "Do you think Penney knew what a hospice nurse is? Seems like murder is a weird accusation against someone who takes care of dying people."

Tran shrugged, then made a left turn. "I suppose it's pretty uncommon for hospice patients to get better."

The barbed wire that had run along beside them for most of their ride gave way to a white, three board fence. Horses grazed in large paddocks. One of the fields was sprinkled with huge logs, big wooden boxes, and a small pond with a boat and a palisade, sans sharp points, on the banks. Back off the road, there was a fieldstone house and a large red barn. There were some other constructions around the barn, but PC wasn't able to tell if they were arenas or pens from where she was sitting.

Tran pulled into the drive and pressed the intercom button on the security keypad.

"Bucephalus."

"Possumwood PD," Tran replied.

The gate slowly swung open, and he pulled through, continuing down the caliche drive to the house. When they got out of the car, a woman holding a lead rope attached to a tall horse stood at the front of the barn. PC estimated the woman's height at about 5'4". The top of the horse's shoulder was probably another four or five inches above her head.

She patted the horse's neck. "I'm Stacey." She turned and called down the barn aisle, "Becca? Can you come get Calypso and put him in the round pen?"

"Morning, Ms. Clemmons. I'm Officer Tran and this is Detective Donovan. We'd like—"

"Hold that thought. We can go in my office in just a sec."

A tall, willowy young woman with midnight hair emerged from the barn and led the horse away.

"Follow me." The horsewoman led the way down the barn aisle. A breezeway bisected the corridor about midway down, opening it up for a cross-flow of fresh air. Two of the corner rooms sported a closed door. Of the two corner spaces that did not have standard interior doors, one appeared to be a feed room and the other looked like a place for horses to stand, probably to be groomed or saddled.

Stacey opened the door with a window and invited them inside. A bay window at the back of the room looked out onto a riding arena. A small office desk squatted near the window and three red folding chairs were arranged haphazardly in front. Stacey went behind the desk and sat, gesturing toward the chairs.

"How can I help you this morning?"

"Yes, ma'am. Thank you for taking the time." Tran leaned forward in his chair.

"This is a beautiful place you have here, Ms. Clemmons." PC looked around the office. Pictures of glossy horses with large competition ribbons hanging from their bridles covered the walls. A glass case held an assortment of trophies.

"Thanks, but I'm very short on time, so could we cut to the chase?"

"Of course." PC folded her hands in her lap. "Did you know Bradford Penney?"

Stacey's shoulders slumped and her eyes rolled up to the ceiling for a moment. She shook her head. "That man is crazy. I almost had to get a restraining order against him. Still might. What's he done now?"

"Died." Tran's answer was quick and to the point.

The horse trainer's hand flew to her mouth. "Oh, wow. Was he murdered?"

Tran raised an eyebrow. "Why do you ask that?"

"If he died in his sleep, you wouldn't be here. I can't say I'm surprised. What happened?"

PC straightened. "He was found in a vat of Oktoberfest lager at the Biersal."

Stacey fidgeted with a pen. "Poor Ken must be beside himself."

"Ken Zimmerman?" PC sucked her teeth.

"Yes."

"Why is that?" Tran asked.

Stacey's lip quirked upward, as if she were surprised they didn't know. "Ken's daughter boards a horse out here. She's outgrown him, so we had gone to look at a new prospect, and I dropped her and her mother off at the Biersal. It was on the way back to the farm—I'd picked them up there on the way out. When we walked in, Ken and that Penney guy were having a knock-down drag out shouting match. Penney said people were saying that the barley in the brewing area was infested with rats, and it was only a matter of time before someone got typhus, or plague, or something. Ken told him to get out and if he ever came back, he'd personally see to it that Penney never harassed anyone again."

Chapter 6

PC AND TRAN turned to look at each other.

Tran cleared his throat. "When was this?"

Stacey appeared to be doing arithmetic on her fingers. "Thursday."

"Yes, well, we'll have to talk to him about that." PC shifted in her seat and crossed her ankles. "I understand you had your own confrontation with Mr. Penney."

The horse trainer groaned. "That man, I swear. So, my horse, Piglet, and I won the three star at North Georgia in September. I was really excited. Put it on all my socials. Then, about two weeks ago, I came in from the cross-country field with the whole group of riders I'd been schooling out there, and here is this weirdo in my feed room. I called the cops," her eyes cut to Tran, "but he bailed before they got here. He said he was looking for the steroids I must have given my horse."

Tran squinted. "First of all, would you explain to me what a three star is?"

"It's an international level three-day event. Dressage, cross-country, and show jumping. They're rated from one to five stars, depending on how hard they are."

PC didn't feel like she knew much more after that explanation than she had before.

Her expression must have showed that, because Stacey stood up and pointed to a picture of a rider in a double-breasted coat with tails on a white horse prancing in the sand. "Dressage." Her hand moved one picture over. The same horse was now in mid-air over a heart-stopping ditch and hedge obstacle. "Cross-country." She pointed to the last of the three in that group—the white horse clearing a stack of blue and white striped poles, with a rider dressed in a black blazer and tight, white pants. "Show jumping."

"Did you see him again after that?" PC asked.

"Yes. I got an alert from the motion-activated security camera. That man was trying to get into the barn, but when the lights came on, he ran off."

"So, I have another question about your horse show," Tran's hands flopped into an open gesture. "Just for the sake of argument, if you were giving your horse steroids, what would be the consequences?"

"Oh, wow. I'd be disqualified from my win. But they take random samples of all the entrants and drug test the top three winners at the show, and Piglet was clean. Unless my vet had a really good reason to prescribe them, I would never give her anabolic steroids—they can make horses really dangerous to handle. And it could get me banned from showing, either temporarily or permanently."

"And that would be bad for your training business, right?" PC asked.

"Oh, yeah. Good clients would flee and I don't want to even think about the kind of people that reputation would attract."

The office door banged open, and the young woman who'd taken the horse earlier shouted, "Spring is loose!"

Stacey jumped up and ran toward the door. "Sorry, I have to go!" she mumbled as she raced out.

"I guess we're dismissed." PC stood up. "Another two star?"

"One and a half."

They walked down the long barn aisle to Tran's cruiser. PC heard the crunch of hoof on gravel before she saw the horse, white with little brown speckles, career around the corner. He sidestepped and pivoted away from them.

Straight toward Tran's car.

There was no way he could stop—he was too close.

PC braced for a wreck.

Instead, the horse tucked up his front legs and sailed over the hood of the car as if it were a minor inconvenience. He gave a few victory bucks, then, tail raised like a hairy flag, galloped away.

Appearing from the other side of the barn, Stacey and her assistant trailed far behind in a golf cart as he headed toward greener pastures.

Tran shook his head as he unlocked his squad. "Glad that's not my job."

PC got in and buckled her seatbelt, and they were soon headed back to town. She drummed her fingers on the vinyl underneath the window. "Do you think it's worth talking to Daphne Jones?"

"I guess it wouldn't hurt. I doubt we'll find much useful information, but it's not like we've got anything else to do. Except find Ken Zimmerman."

Fred and Daphne Jones' house was a tidy Craftsman just south of downtown. Curtains over the open windows fluttered in the breeze. Tran knocked on the screen door.

"Just a minute," came from inside.

A woman PC guessed to be in her sixties cracked open the door. "May I help you?"

"I'm Officer Tran from the Possumwood PD, and this is Detective Donovan. May we come in?"

"That was fast." She swung the door wide and waved them inside.

PC wiped her feet on the mat. "You were expecting us?"

"Of course. I just called about the clothes stolen from my line about five minutes ago. Didn't expect you to get here so quickly." She continued through the house until she arrived at the back door. "Out there. They took every last sock on the line. Unbelievable."

PC and Tran stepped into the yard. While he radioed in his location at the complainant's residence, she looked around. Sheets flapped at one end of the line, and male and female garments filled the rest, with a few gaps along the way. The yard was fenced with four-foot-tall chain link. It wouldn't have been hard for someone to have climbed over. But why? First quilts at the Afters, now socks at the nurse's.

Tran searched the backyard for any obvious clues, like footprints. PC spoke with Mrs. Jones.

"Ma'am, do you have any kind of doorbell or security camera?"

Daphne sagged in her chair. "No, we don't."

"It's a gorgeous day to have off work."

"I work the night shift. I'm usually asleep this time of day. Fred had hung out the laundry before he left for work, but he heard on the radio it was supposed to rain, so he called me. Left at 7:30. Called a little before 9:00."

"Mrs. Jones, these two things may not be related. Just as likely, they aren't. But did you have an altercation with Bradford Penney recently?"

She pinched the bridge of her nose and closed her eyes. "Poor Brad. People often struggle with death. They feel like there has to be a reason or someone to blame. Bodies die. It happens to every single one of us, sooner or later. Brad's mother had a stroke. It was both unexpected and catastrophic. Really knocked him for a loop.

We did the best we could for her, but she wasn't aware of what was happening."

"I see."

"Not a hundred percent sure you do. Do you know what terminal lucidity is?"

PC shook her head. "No."

"It's not an uncommon thing. A patient will be semi-conscious or unresponsive for some time, then all of a sudden, they sit up and seem to be fine. I've seen them last as long as three days after, but typically, they die within hours. When Paisley sat up, smiled, and said she needed her suitcase, Brad was sure she'd spontaneously recovered."

"Can't really blame him."

Daphne rubbed her forehead. "That's the worst part. Families get their hopes up. But I knew she was about to pass. It was so obvious to me."

PC shifted her weight. "Why?"

"Even more common than terminal lucidity is where the patient says they need to get ready, because they have to catch a train, or a bus, or a taxi. I've been a hospice nurse twenty years. I've seen people recover twice, but I have never seen anyone who starts 'getting ready' last more than a day."

"So he thought his mother was recovering, then she died, so you must have killed her."

"He lashed out at me because he couldn't accept his mother's death. I'm not happy he did that, but I understand he's going through some trauma."

Tran came back to the porch. "I'm sorry, ma'am. I took down some notes for my file, but I didn't find anything conclusive. We'll advise you when we make any progress on your case." He handed her a quarter sheet of paper with some check boxes and the case number handwritten on it.

"Thanks." She set the page on top of a low bookshelf. "Do you think Brad Penney might have stolen our socks?"

Tran blinked a couple of times. "No, ma'am. I'm certain that he didn't."

Daphne looked at PC then back to Tran. "Why's that?"

"Mr. Penney is deceased."

Her eyes narrowed as she turned to PC. "You could have told me."

"I'm sorry, ma'am."

The nurse led them to the door, and they left. Halfway to the station, Tran slapped his hip. "Oh, man."

"What's wrong?"

"I grabbed my flashlight to look under the porch. I must have left it in the back yard."

He swung the car around and headed toward the Jones' house. When they arrived, a car that hadn't been there a few minutes before was in the driveway.

PC unbuckled. "I'll go get it. Be right back."

As she got near the front door, the detective clearly saw through one of the open windows. Daphne Jones stood there speaking with a man. It took PC a moment to recognize Joaquin Jones, the bartender from the *Silver Dollar Saloon* at the *Best Southern Motel*.

He rubbed his jaw. "Okay. I got rid of it, just like you told me. Now what do I do?"

Chapter 7

THE NEXT-DOOR NEIGHBOR's dog barked as PC put her foot on the first step. Joaquin and Daphne both turned toward her and must have seen her through the window. Daphne opened the door before she even knocked.

"Is there something else I can help you with, Detective?"

"Sorry to bother you, ma'am. Officer Tran left his flashlight on your back porch. I came back to retrieve it."

Daphne stepped aside to let her in. Joaquin was gone. PC forced her breathing into a slow, regular rhythm as adrenalin trickled into her bloodstream. Joaquin could be anywhere inside. Would he remain concealed, or jump out and attack?

A floorboard creaked under her foot, and she flinched, head whipping around to check for danger. She walked through the house and opened the back door. Daphne stood on the porch, supervising. It was a completely normal thing for Daphne to do, but it made PC nervous.

The detective stepped out into the grass and was never so happy to see a metal flashlight. It stood on its end on the edge of the deck, obscured from the front by one of the pillars that held up the roof of the porch.

She picked it up and waved it at Daphne. "Thank you, ma'am."

Daphne didn't speak as they walked back through the house, but when she opened the door, she said, "Have a good day, Detective."

"You, too, ma'am. You, too."

PC memorized the license plate number on the car in the driveway and wrote it down as Tran drove off.

"What's that about?"

"As I was coming up on the porch, I saw Joaquin Jones through the open window, and he told Daphne, 'I got rid of it like you told me. Now what do I do?' Joaquin wasn't in the living room when I came in, but I'm sure he was hiding in the house somewhere. He did *not* want me to see him."

"That does sound suspicious, but it could have been anything. Maybe a cat?"

"A cat? And he hid out of shame for casting out an adoring feline?"

"When you put it that way... It does sound sketchy, but there's nothing to relate it to Penney's death."

"You aren't wrong."

"So what's Daphne's suspect star rating?"

"One."

"I agree that she probably didn't kill him with her own fair hand. But she might be an accessory."

"Her own fair hand? That sounds very artsy-fartsy. What's with the colorful language?"

It does sound exactly like something Drew would say. "I think that's just a pigment of your imagination."

"We've moved on to dad jokes now?"

PC squelched a smile. "So, what do you make of Daphne's story about finding Ken and Penney going at it in the Biersal on Thursday?"

"Makes Ken's disappearance look incriminating. He threatens Penney on Thursday night, Penney turns up dead Saturday evening, and Ken vanishes without his cell phone. People who don't want to be located have a habit of doing that."

PC sighed. "Yeah, I hear what you're saying. But Ken Zimmerman, of all people? He always seemed so level-headed and… common sensical."

"Is that a real word?"

"Did you know what I meant?"

Tran rolled his eyes.

PC ran her tongue over her teeth. "But there's always a straw that breaks the camel's back. Did Penney pack on that straw?"

"I guess we need to talk with his wife about it, since Daphne said she also witnessed the confrontation."

The detective snorted. "Penney seemed to be fond of confrontation. I mean, he went after a bunch of people. He accused Abike Sabo of immigration fraud, the Reynolds women of manufacturing ghosts, Stacy Clemmons of juicing her horse, and Daphne Jones of killing his mother. There's no proof to any of that."

"But if the rumors got out and folks believed them…"

"It wouldn't matter if they were true. And all of those people could lose their livelihoods. Don't forget Abike's a refugee, so if she was deported, her life would be at risk."

"True, but right now, I'm leaning toward Zimmerman."

PC sighed. "I agree that the circumstantial evidence looks grim, but I don't know… just doesn't feel right." She looked out the window. "I seem to remember Mama saying something about Penney getting ready to break a major story in that article about the Social Security case. Where the husband died…?"

"Yep. The feds are looking into that. We're getting a warrant for Penney's cell phone data. Gotta check out his office, hope his computer isn't password protected, and look at his files."

"He said it would rock the entire town. Something bad about the Biersal fits that bill. But the same is true about any of the other Possumwood institutions."

Keryn Zimmerman sat at her kitchen table, holding a mug of hot tea as if it was a shield.

PC put her hands on the table. "Mrs. Zimmerman, I know this is a difficult time for you. Are you aware of any conflict between your husband and Mr. Bradford Penney?"

"Ken did not kill that man. He could be in danger right now from the real killer, and you don't care." Keryn glowered.

Tran's hand twitched, as if he were going to reach out and touch her but stopped himself. "We're doing everything we can to find your husband. Extra Possumwood officers are on patrol, the Mirabella County Sheriff has eyes out, and even the state troopers are on the alert."

Keryn's lips pursed. "So you can arrest him for murder. I told Elwood it was all a misunderstanding. Ken will go down there and get it straightened out as soon as he gets back."

PC tilted her head. "Have you spoken to your husband since Saturday?"

"Maybe I have. Maybe I haven't. But before he says anything to the police, he's gonna talk to our lawyer. That's just common sense."

But only if he knows the police are looking for him. She has had contact with him.

The detective deliberately slowed her breathing and moved her hands nearer to Keryn. "You're right. Your husband is definitely what we call a person of interest. But we're not automatically assuming he's involved in the crime. He may know something helpful. He could have seen someone or witnessed some event that would break the investigation wide open. Perhaps *you* know something that might help?"

The mug of tea clunked on the table as Keryn set it down. She swallowed and stared into the cup, perhaps hoping to read the leaves. "There was an incident on Thursday. Kelsey—that's our daughter—and I had been out all day and got dropped off at the pub. Our friend came in with us to get some pretzels. I was so embarrassed. When we arrived, Brad Penney was there, accusing Ken of allowing a rat infestation in the brewing area. That brewery is cleaner than my house!"

PC glanced around the immaculate kitchen. She hadn't noticed any evidence of rats on the truncated tour of the brewery last night.

"Anyway," Keryn continued. "Ken told him he was out of his mind. I told Bradford Penney that if there was a rat in the Biersal, it was him. He just laughed at that, then said that he was also investigating rats at the Best Southern, and soon folks would know who had the worst infestation. Then he left." She shook her head. "I didn't know him well, but I think his mother's death last month must have broken him. He just seemed… I hate to say 'crazed,' perhaps that's too strong of a word, but I can't think of a better one."

"That's very helpful, Mrs. Zimmerman." PC glanced at Tran. "What time did your husband leave to go to the Biersal yesterday morning? Did he tell you his plans for the day?"

Keryn eyed Tran. "Y'all already asked me that. I don't normally get out of bed until seven, but Ken usually gets up around six. The glycol unit had been acting up, and he wanted to get it repaired before the festivities started. He did not inform me of any travel plans at that time."

But perhaps he told you later. "Do you know if the repairs were completed?" PC chewed the inside of her cheek.

"I don't. Ken seemed to think it had a short, or possibly a clog in the pump, because it would work fine for a while, then make a terrible noise and stop, then it would start up again. Thank goodness the weather's been chilly enough that it's easy to keep the temperatures right without a lot of mechanical cooling."

The detective looked at Tran. He stood up. "Thank you, Mrs. Zimmerman for taking the time. We'll do our best to bring your husband home safely."

Keryn nodded.

PC also got to her feet. "Thank you, ma'am."

They showed themselves out.

Once they were in the car, PC said, "I'm pretty sure she's talked to her husband, even if she doesn't know where he is."

"You think we should invite her in for a more formal interview?"

The detective shook her head. "Not at this time. But if Ken doesn't turn up by tomorrow afternoon…"

Tran pulled onto the street. "Where to?"

"I think it's very interesting that Joaquin Jones, who works at the *Silver Dollar Saloon* was getting rid of something on the q.t. and Penney said he was looking into a rat infestation at the *Best Southern Motel.*"

"We should talk to Mr. Jones."

Tran got his address and they stopped by his apartment, but he didn't answer the door. His car wasn't in the parking lot, either. They drove by the bedraggled *Best Southern Motel*, but the lounge wasn't open on a Sunday morning. A rodent metropolis at the run-down building was a strong possibility—she shuddered at the memory of having a huge roach fly at her during an investigation there. But how would a rat report about this dive rock the town?

Probably wouldn't even raise an eyebrow, just elicit a 'well, duh' reaction. *What am I missing?*

They were within two blocks of the station when Tran's radio crackled.

"Zebra-230. Do you copy?"

"10-4. This is Zebra-230."

"10-19. 10-19 ASAP. Your missing person is at the station."

Chapter 8

"WHAT?" PC COCKED her head.

"10-77. Be there in two minutes." Tran replied to the radio mic.

"What do you think happened? He turned himself in? Got picked up somewhere?"

He pulled into a parking space. "Guess we're about to find out."

They exited the car, and Tran swiped his card to open the back door. They bee-lined it for the holding area, but no one was there.

"Interrogation?" PC asked.

Tran nodded, and they headed that way. PC peered through the long, narrow window into the broom-closet-sized interrogation room to see a tall man speaking with Ken Zimmerman. It took PC a minute to figure out it was Woody. He'd gotten his hair buzzed so short it almost counted as having his head shaved. His arm was thrown over the back of the chair and his legs were stretched out as if he planned to be in there visiting for a while.

"I'm going to get some coffee. Want me to bring you anything, Tran?"

"I'm good, thanks."

PC stifled a yawn and meandered to the break room for some perk-up juice. When she returned, Woody was still in the interrogation room with Ken. *If only they had a camera and a microphone...*

The detective had just about decided to go sit in the conference room—her makeshift office when she was at the department—to wait. She might be able to distract herself with cold case files for a little while.

The door opened and Woody stepped out, closing it behind him.

"Mornin' Donovan."

PC glanced at her FlitBit. It was five minutes until midday. "Morning." She tried not to stare at his shorn head. "So, what's the story?"

"Well, Ken says that he arrived at the Biersal at 6:30 AM to try and fix the glycol machine. He realized that the problem was with the ball valve actuator, whatever that is. He looked at ordering one from his regular vendor in New Orleans, but it was Saturday and there wouldn't be anyone in the shipping department to overnight it until Monday, so he wouldn't get it until Tuesday afternoon. He bought one over the phone and they said they'd leave it with the security guard for him to pick up Saturday afternoon, because he couldn't get there before they closed at noon."

The detective raised her coffee cup. "He didn't notice his phone was gone?"

"When he stopped for gas, he went to call Keryn, and realized his cell was missing, figured he'd left it at the brewery. He arrived in New Orleans, picked up the part, then checked into his hotel around two in the afternoon. Says he intended to call his wife when he got to his room but fell asleep. When he woke up, it was four AM. He checked out of the room and drove back to Possumwood, stopping to eat breakfast along the way. He called Keryn then, and she told him what was going on, so he came here."

"How long does it take to drive from Possumwood to New Orleans?"

Woody weighed air with his palms as the scale. "If you drive straight through... about six hours. More if you hit traffic in Houston or Beaumont."

"There's always traffic in Houston, but it's usually not too bad early on a Saturday morning. What time did he say he left?"

"Between 7 and 7:30. He's got receipts from the gas station, hotel, and the valve thing itself. I'm going to cut him loose. Got no reason to keep him."

PC tapped a thumb on her coffee cup. "When Tran and I visited with Daphne Jones, we left, then returned briefly. Joaquin Jones was there, and I heard him say he'd gotten rid of something. Don't know what it was, but it did sound suspicious—he didn't want us to see him there, because he hid somewhere in the house when I came in. Have you gotten any results on that crowbar from the dumpster, Woody?"

"We sent it to Harris County Forensics. They haven't examined it yet, but those red flecks looked like rust to me."

"It was in a dumpster from the hardware store, so that wouldn't be too surprising," Tran said.

Woody rubbed his head. "Why don't you track down Jones and see what his story is?"

"On it." Tran took a step toward the back door.

PC tossed her styro cup in the trash. "Later."

The detective closed the car door and buckled her seatbelt. "When did the chief get his new 'do?"

Tran backed out of the parking slot. "Last week. Said it was getting patchy, so he may as well mow it."

PC nodded. "So, where are we going first?"

"Let's try Jones' apartment again. Silver Dollar doesn't open until three, if I remember correctly."

They drove around the twenty-four-unit apartment complex and didn't see his car. The boxy, pre-cast concrete design and decorative concrete screen blocks gave the six buildings—four units each—a 1960s motel look. The construction was probably about as old as PC. Still, they were well-kept and clean. A few yellow leaves in the ash trees echoed the bright rows of orange and yellow mums that edged the walkway.

"We may as well try it." PC turned toward Tran. "He might have a roommate."

Tran backed the car into a visitor parking space, and they got out. "Let's see what happens."

They climbed the iron and concrete stairs that rattled with every step to the second floor. After locating Jones' apartment, Tran smiled at PC and knocked.

"Hang on." A muffled male voice came from inside.

Moments later, the door swung open and a young man wearing nothing but a towel and a rose in his teeth stood inside.

"Uh." Tran took a step back.

"Uh." The rose dropped onto the floor as the man's jaw opened.

"I take it you were expecting someone else?" PC asked.

"Yeah… um. Is… there something I can help you with?"

Tran peered over the scantily clad man's shoulder. "Is Joaquin Jones here?"

"No, haven't seen him all day, but I just got up a few minutes ago."

PC gave him a practiced smile. "May we come in and talk to you for a minute, Mr…?"

"Sure." He checked the walkway, then stepped back. "I'm Tim Calloway."

Tran and PC entered the apartment. It was cluttered, but not dirty. A half-empty cup of something milky sat on the battered coffee table, next to a cell phone.

"I just got out of the shower. Let me go put on some pants right quick."

"Of course," PC said pleasantly.

He hurried into a bedroom. A drawer opened and closed. Then another. Plastic hangers clattered. Calloway returned wearing cargo shorts and a polo. "Can I... get you anything to drink? Oatmeal pie?" He gestured to an open box of snack cakes on the dining room table.

"No, thank you. We'd like to ask you a few questions. Shouldn't take long."

"About?"

PC sat on the couch. "Is Joaquin your roommate?"

"Yeah. Is he in some kind of trouble?" He perched on the edge of the love seat, perpendicular to the detective.

"We just want to talk to him." PC nodded. "When was the last time you saw him?"

Tran wandered around the small apartment while Tim and PC spoke.

"Well, I spent the night at my girlfriend's house Friday. I got home around noon Saturday. He wasn't here. It was almost two in the afternoon when he showed up. He was running late for work, so he stripped down and dropped his clothes in the basket..." Tim gestured to a plastic clothes hamper near the stacked washer and dryer in the kitchen. "Threw on his work clothes and left. Haven't seen him since."

Tran moseyed over to the laundry area. "PC? You might want to take a look at this."

"What is it?" The detective got up and joined her colleague.

Right on top of the basket of Joaquin Jones' clothes lay a bloody tee-shirt.

Chapter 9

PC TRIED NOT to gape at the blood-smeared garment. "Is that the shirt Joaquin took off yesterday?"

Tim Calloway scurried over to the laundry basket and his eyes got big as basketballs. "Yeah. I, uh… I didn't notice…"

Tran exchanged a look with PC. "Mr. Calloway? Do we have your permission to look around the apartment?"

"Yeah. Sure. Whatever you want."

Tran radioed for more officers. The apartment was searched and photographed. Save for a bloody towel in Joaquin's room, they discovered nothing other than the gory shirt. PC and Tran transported the blood-soaked materials to Dr. Mack for analysis.

The Medical Examiner gloved up and carefully laid the fabric on a steel table. He picked up a swab and squirted a clear liquid on it. "Now, this is the Kastle Meyer, or phenolphthalein test. If this swab turns pink, it's most likely blood."

He rubbed the wet cotton over Joaquin's shirt, then added a squirt from a bottle labeled 'hydrogen peroxide.'

It wasn't instantaneous, but a purply-pink hue soon darkened the swab.

Dr. Mack used another swab for the towel with the same results.

Tran cleared his throat. "Okay, now that you've confirmed it's blood, can you get DNA?"

"Of course, of course. But let's not be hasty. It's *probably* blood—there are a few known substances that can give a false positive—but before we spend your annual investigative budget on DNA tests, how about we confirm that it's *human* blood?"

PC glanced at the shirt and towel. "An Ouchterlony test?"

"Exactly. It has to incubate overnight, so we'll know in the morning. I'll give you a call when it's ready."

A plate of sizzling fajitas passed by, and PC's stomach growled like an angry bear. She dipped a tortilla chip in house-made, secret recipe salsa. *Jillibella's is* almost *as good as Hermano de Felix back home in the Heights.* The chip crunched between her teeth and the complex salsa spread over her tongue. She was almost too hungry to enjoy the roasted red peppers, simmered tomatoes, and the jalapeno kick.

"Do you think he did it?" Tran stirred his tea.

PC finished chewing and swallowed. "Joaquin?"

"Yeah."

"Well. Ken Zimmerman seemed like the most logical suspect for a while. But now that's a harder case to make. Brad Penney was investigating the Best Southern. There was a plastic cocktail sword at the death scene, and Joaquin is a bartender at the *Silver Dollar Saloon*. He was out all morning Saturday and returned with a bloody shirt. Penney was struck on the head with a flat, heavy object. Scalp wounds bleed a lot. Circumstantial evidence doesn't seem to be in his favor. But there's still the crowbar from the dumpster where Drew and I found Abike Sabo."

"Chief said he thought those spots were rust." Tran sipped his tea.

"Might be, but that doesn't mean there isn't blood on it."

"True. When we spoke with Abike Saturday night, she was at the clinic checking on some animals. Said she was at work at 7 AM on Saturday. Her coworkers confirmed. Even if that crowbar is the murder weapon, I think it's a weird coincidence that it was in the dumpster she got her arm trapped in." Tran scooped up guacamole with a chip.

That's how Abike knew that Penney was dead—she'd already talked to the police by the time we found her.

PC sipped her tea. "You know… might not be a coincidence. If you were driving from the Biersal to the Best Southern, Justice Hardware is on the way."

"You're right."

"What bothers me, though, is if Ken didn't kill Penney, what was the killer doing in the Biersal's brewery? We believe that Penney had an appointment with Ken at some point, and it's weird that Stan appears not to be aware of the Thursday night fight. Did someone pick up a crowbar and follow Penney inside? After all, no one mentioned a break-in at the brewery."

The server brought their food, and they put the case discussion on pause until she left.

The detective rolled some rice and beans into a warm tortilla. "I hate to think of this as a scenario, but what if Stan didn't mention it because he didn't want to draw attention to the kerfuffle and didn't think we'd find out? What if Ken invited Penney to the brewery on the pretext of disproving the rat rumor? Stan hit him from behind and they lifted him into the vat. Then Ken left to draw suspicion away from Stan and give himself an alibi in New Orleans?"

"I suppose it could have happened that way. But do you think they'd ruin all that beer by dumping a body into it? How much does that production loss cost them? Especially when this story Penney was pushing was easily disproved."

"I think you're right, if the rat story is all there is to it."

"And don't forget there are a few others who haven't been completely ruled out. I mean, Justice Hardware is also between the Biersal and Stacey Clemmons' place."

They stopped talking and focused on the hot food. Before long, their plates were empty and the checks paid.

The server returned with their credit cards. PC stood up and rubbed her stomach. "I shouldn't have had such a big lunch this late. I'm meeting Drew for dinner at *Truffles!* later."

"You seem to be spending a lot of time together."

"You don't spend time with your friends?"

"My friends are too cheap to go to fancy restaurants."

PC gave a little laugh. "Just a heads up. I can help you tomorrow, but not Tuesday. It's the seventh."

"What's special about the seventh?"

PC rubbed her eyes. "It's the anniversary of my dad's murder. Mama always goes to the cemetery for a remembrance. I've gone with her as often as I could, but didn't make every one of them, especially right after I left home."

"Of course. I'm sorry."

PC woke up when the rain started in the wee hours of Tuesday morning. It didn't stop until almost lunchtime, and the Donovan family got a later start to *Big Cypress Cemetery* than they usually did on Trey's death-day anniversary.

Mama had started this bittersweet ritual so that we'd never forget our father. Bring fresh flowers to the grave, spend some time in silence, then each person shares a memory. I honestly don't know if this makes it better or worse. Wounds never heal if you keep picking at the scab.

PC laid down a plastic tarp on the concrete bench at the end of Trey Donovan's grave, and Rose and Daisy sat. The detective stood next to her mother.

A dandelion had grown at the base of the headstone. Rocky plucked the stem and the fluffy head was shorn of seeds that parachuted into the breeze, wild wishes on the wind.

PC watched them fly. *I wish I could solve Daddy's murder…*

The bouquet of white roses and baby's breath that Rose had placed in the cemetery vase stood in stark relief against the black granite of the double tombstone, Trey's name and dates of birth and death on one side, hers on the other, save the final date.

Rose cleared her throat. "Do y'all remember Muffin, the white cat? Your daddy was dead set against bringin' her in the house. I went to Marberger's to get some kitten chow, and when I came back, she was curled up in his lap, purrin' to beat the band. He wouldn't move because she was so dang comfortable. Took her no time to work her feline wiles on him."

PC sighed, remembering that day—she was probably eight years old and Daisy six—when they found the tiny grey kitten wandering in the street, meowing. They knew their father wasn't interested in having pets in the house, so they snuck Muffin inside to the room they shared. After a bath, it turned out the grey kitten was actually white. And hungry.

Rocky cleared his throat. "Remember that year I thought I was gonna have a pen of chickens for the county fair?"

Daisy chuckled.

He smiled at his sister. "Me and Daddy built the coop together. Chickens got sifted. But I guess we done a good enough job on the construction, 'cuz Mama's still usin' it to this day."

Rocky was supposed to have been raising broilers, but he ordered laying hens instead, so once they got to the fair, the judges rejected them. But he'd taken the chickens back home and that's probably where Mama got her chicken addiction. Also true that Daddy could eat omelets three meals a day.

Daisy smiled. "Y'all remember my twelfth birthday? I had that roller skatin' party in Horice? Nadine and I was too scared to get out on the floor, so Daddy took us each by the hand and led us along the outside edge of the rink. He got fussed at by the manager 'cause he was out there with no skates. But once he'd gotten us going, we held on to the wall and stayed on our feet. Think I even got about halfway around without holdin' on by the end of the party."

Daisy hadn't roller skated before or since. But that was the occasion PC and Woody had gotten together as a couple. They'd known each other since kindergarten. But like Daisy, PC battled with the skates that had seemed to have individual minds of their own. Woody wasn't doing much better, but they held on to each other and struggled around the rink. After the cake had been served and presents opened, he'd offered to help carry Daisy's loot out to the car. PC had held the door, and he'd given her a quick, chaste kiss when no one was looking.

My turn. What's a story I can tell? When Woody dumped me two days before the Homecoming Dance, Daddy took me on a walk. He told me that right now the wound was fresh and painful, but after a while, when my heart had healed, I'd come to see it as a gift—intentionally or not, Woody was letting me go so that I had the opportunity to find someone who truly loved me. And never seek revenge, Daddy said, because, and he quoted a poem, 'though the mills of the gods grind slowly, they grind exceeding small.' Becoming a detective was my own way of grinding out justice, I suppose. But I never shared this memory with my family, or anyone else.

"So, there was that time that I was learning to drive, and we were out on 720. He told me to shift up to fifth gear, but when I stepped on the clutch, the edge of my shoe caught the brake, too. Only time I remember hearing him swear. It was just as well, because three deer ran out in front of us. If I hadn't slammed on the brakes, it would have been a bad day for everybody." *Sometimes it's better to be lucky than good.*

Rocky snickered. "I remember you still had that mark from hitting your head on the steering wheel for picture day."

PC smiled. It was funny now, with decades of distance.

Rose stood up and walked beside the grave, running her hand over the top of the gravestone as she passed. Rocky, Daisy, and PC followed silently.

They had a subdued family dinner. After Daisy left, PC went to her bedroom early, spending two hours going over and over each page in her copy of Trey Donovan's murder book. No new clues or insights presented themselves.

The photographic enhancement of a reflection in the window appeared to show someone wearing an oversized rodeo trophy belt buckle. Probably half of the people in a twenty-mile radius of downtown Possumwood had at least one of those.

A Colt Python was found buried under a concrete driveway, in a subdivision that was under construction at the time of the murder. The gun was a wildly popular model and PC could think of four people off the top of her head who had owned one, including her father, who had kept it under the counter at the convenience store the family owned. Ballistics testing on the rusty gun had been inconclusive.

In the thirty-nine years since the fatal robbery, all of the original investigators had passed, so there was no one left to talk with and bounce ideas off of.

She slid the binder underneath her bed and turned out the lights. Her mattress was strangely uncomfortable, and she tossed and turned, failing to find a relaxing position. It felt like she had just closed her eyes when the alarm squawked, and she had to get up and feed the critters.

Most of the time, when PC went out to feed in the morning, Rose's rescue crew was waiting for her at the gate. Not this morning. Scruffy beige Guinevere and sleek black Arthur stood haunch to haunch, but Hazel, the three-legged goat, was missing.

The donkeys looked at her but stayed put when she entered the paddock. It was then she noticed a dark form lying on the ground on the other side of the equids.

Hazel, her back to PC, wasn't moving.

Chapter 10

"Hazel?" PC called, not really expecting a reply.

The detective trotted out to help the downed goat. She hurried around the donkeys, giving Guinevere a tickle on her muzzle as she passed.

Hazel lay on her side, one hind foot and one horn tangled in the strings of a mylar balloon bouquet that had gradually given up its helium and drifted onto the ground. She was breathing, but sweaty and shaking. The grass was torn up in long gouges where the goat had raked the earth with sharp hooves in the struggle to free herself.

PC stroked her head. "It's okay, girl. I'm gonna get you out of this."

She ran to the feed room, found the kitchen shears she kept there, and hurried back to Hazel. It only took a few snips to free the goat, who lay flat, exhausted from her fight.

PC called the vet. Dr. Logan would be out soon—he said he'd divert from a vaccination call and see Hazel first.

The detective sat on the ground, cradling the goat's head in her lap, until the doctor and his assistant appeared at the back gate. Cordite belatedly raised the alarm, and PC gently laid Hazel's head on the ground before she rose and scooped the dog up in her arms.

As PC told him what had happened, the veterinarian got out his stethoscope and listened to Hazel's chest, while his tech took her temperature.

"This healed really well." Dr. Logan ran his hand along Hazel's empty shoulder where a leg once extended. "She's a tough girl. I think she'll be fine. Might be stiff and sore for a few days, though."

PC's eyes lingered on the goat's smooth chest. "How did she lose her leg?"

"It was what, six years ago, April?"

"Sounds right," the tech answered.

"Hazel was half-grown, just doing what goats do out in the pasture, when she got bitten by a copperhead. Mrs. Donovan and the farmer brought her in. The farmer was gonna have Hazel euthanized, but Mrs. Donovan said she'd pay for the treatment. It was touch and go. I didn't think Hazel was going to make it. We couldn't save the leg, but miraculously, she survived."

Rose came out the back door and walked across to the wooden fence. She paled when she saw Hazel flat on the ground.

"What happened?" Her voice cracked.

PC gestured toward the pile of spent balloons. "She got tangled up."

Dr. Logan walked toward Rose. "She doesn't seem to be injured, just very stressed. I'm going to give her a shot of B-complex. You can spike her water with molasses to encourage her to drink. I think she'll probably be okay but keep an eye on her. If her temperature becomes elevated, call me ASAP."

Rose covered her mouth with her hand, and she nodded. Tears welled up in her eyes. PC moved to the fence and set the dog down on the other side of the gate before putting an arm around her mother's shoulders. Cordite sat on Rose's feet.

"It's okay, Mama. Dr. Logan was telling me what a fighter baby Hazel was when she lost her leg. She's tough."

Mmmaaammmaaaaaaaa.

Hazel struggled to her feet. Guinevere walked over and sniffed her.

"I'd better get her that injection." The vet turned toward the livestock.

April handed him a syringe containing a bright yellow liquid. When he approached Hazel, Gwen pinned her ears and her head snaked out, bared teeth threatening to bite. April made a move to retrieve the box of medical supplies before it got knocked over. The donkey turned her hindquarters to the tech and cocked one leg.

The rattle of a chain made PC turn to see Rose hurrying through the gate.

Great. The last thing we need is for her to get kicked by Guinevere. "Mama! Wait!"

But Rose was already at Gwen's side scratching her neck. The donkey's huge ears flopped forward as her owner spoke to her.

"Gwennie, honey. Dr. Logan is here to help Hazel. He's gonna give her a shot to make her feel better. Thank you for tryin' to protect her."

Arthur came up behind Rose and poked her in the back with his nose. Gwen nuzzled her hands. Rose scratched both donkeys, and the veterinarian quickly pulled up the skin on Hazel's shoulder and gave her the injection.

He put the plastic cap on the needle. "Rose, you are truly the donkey whisperer. I have a call later in the week I may need to bring you along for."

Rose beamed and continued to scratch the donkeys.

"Thanks Dr. Logan. April." PC opened the gate for them.

"You're welcome. And like I said, if Hazel starts to run a fever, call me."

PC shifted her attention to her mother. Rose had fallen a few weeks ago when she'd come out to see her animals. She'd lain on the ground in the rain for three hours. Other than a mild case of hypothermia, she'd been uninjured. PC had been at her regular Wednesday darts game that evening, and she still felt horribly guilty. She wasn't about to leave her mother out here by herself.

Hazel stood with her head down. Her breathing was almost back to normal. The detective tried to imagine her as a carefree young goat playing in the field. *Had she understood what was happening to her after the deadly snake bite? Do animals have near-death experiences?*

That made her think of Daphne, the hospice nurse. *How was she related to Joaquin Jones?*

"You about ready to come in, Mama? I'm working today." PC glanced at her FlitBit. "Supposed to meet Tran at the station in fifteen minutes."

"Fine." Rose lifted each donkey muzzle for a kiss, then she moved to Hazel. She ran a hand along the goat's back. Hazel winced and raised her head when Rose's fingers met the bulge of the vitamin injection.

"Sorry, honey." She scratched the goat's forehead and around her horns. Hazel's eyes closed.

After a final pat, Rose toddled toward PC and the gate. Rocky was off work today, so hopefully he'd shoulder some of the goat monitoring load.

PC looked out the window of Tran's squad as downtown Possumwood rolled by. Businesses had started putting up decorations for Halloween. There was orange and black tinsel here, green and purple lights there. Cartoonish ghosts, friendly witches, and angry black cats—tails a-flue-brushed—graced shop windows. Pumpkins and plastic jack-o'-lanterns had popped up like mushrooms after a rain. PC smiled, suddenly more in the mood for the ghost tour coming up on Saturday at the Afters.

Tran turned into the parking lot of the small office building on Independence Avenue that housed the offices of the *Possumwood Press*. "We finally got in touch with his son to notify him of the death. He told us where to look for the passwords that Mr. Penney kept on a sheet of paper."

Tran jangled the keys and opened the door. The cluttered office looked as if there had been an explosion in a sticky note factory. Brightly colored squares of paper were stuck on the walls, the computer monitor, and most surfaces of the desk. While Tran searched for the password cheat sheet and woke the computer, PC wandered around the room. Aside from all the sticky notes, there were several framed pictures on the wall.

The first in the group of three was a faded Polaroid of a young man, possibly Penney, standing knee-deep in turquoise water, his arm around a young woman in a yellow bikini. A palm tree cast a shadow across white beach sand in the foreground.

Inches away, another photo of the couple, slightly older—the man sported a patchy mustache—with a baby this time. They were standing on a rocky overlook, a metal plaque to their right. Mountains rose in the distance behind them, the tallest ones capped with snow.

The next wall sported a framed newspaper clipping from the society page of an unnamed newspaper. A light-haired woman with an impressive bouffant hairdo stood next to a tall, handsome man with dark hair and black-framed glasses. She wore an elegant white lace bridal gown, and he cut a dashing figure in a tux and bow tie. The headline read, "Paisley Elaine Penney, Daughter of Noted Local Restauranteurs Herman and Lola Penney, Weds Stephen Bradford Hirsch of Amarillo."

Tucked into a corner of the frame was a 5 x 7 of an elderly couple in front of a stunning gold and white cake topped with a triumphant wax or ceramic '50.' They looked much older than fifty years, so it was probably a fiftieth wedding anniversary. PC took snapshots of the pictures in case she wanted to review them later.

"Found it!" Tran shook a piece of paper over his head.

He sat in the office chair at the computer. PC moved a delicate blown-glass jack-o'-lantern out of the way and leaned against the desk. Tran opened up Penney's document folder.

Oh, boy. This may take a while. It looked like a hundred sub-folders just on the visible part of the screen and those only went down to the beginning of 'F'—no telling how many there were after that.

PC rifled through files in the credenza behind the desk. All of those seemed business-related. The lease contract. Various bills. Bank statements. PC looked at the most recent one, but it raised no suspicions. There was more cash in than out, but Penney wasn't getting rich.

The detective found two thick envelopes marked with the 'House SA' on one and 'House Possumwood' on the other. Bradford Penney had just sold a house he'd owned for twenty-nine years in San Antonio and bought one in Possumwood.

She sighed and started sifting through the mountain of papers on the desk.

A slip of paper with some handwriting on it caught her eye, and she paused to give it a closer look.

Tran turned his head slightly. "Find anything interesting?"

"Maybe. There's a note here. Says 'Rat Hunter. Best cheese? Biersal.' Does that refer to his meeting with Ken Zimmerman?"

"Sounds like it."

"What about you? Anything good?"

"Not sure. He's researched horse steroids and racing, Killer nurses. Hospice agreements. Rat-borne illness. Lots of research on organized crime generally and one case from about thirty years ago in Dallas specifically."

"Defendant?"

"Andre Thibodeaux, originally from Shreveport. Confidential informant gave him up. He got life. Racketeering, conspiracy to commit murder, wire fraud, mail fraud, and tax evasion."

"If tax evasion was good enough for Al Capone, it should be good enough for Andre Thibodeaux. I guess."

Then she noticed the name of the article's writer: Steve Hirsch. *That guy?* She scrunched her nose and contemplated the framed newspaper clipping for a moment. *Wonder why he kept all his research on this one case?*

They continued to search the office but didn't find any stand-out clues to why someone might want to kill Bradford Penney. He could be abrasive, but according to the receipts in his email, he donated monthly to the Bateman Children's Hospital in Dallas.

PC got out her notepad and jotted down the name of the hospital and also the names 'Andre Thibodeaux' and 'Stephen Hirsch.' She'd look into those when they returned to the station.

Tran locked the door, and they got into his cruiser. PC plucked a few brown goat hairs off of her pants. "Daphne Jones. Do you think she and Joaquin worked together to kill Brad Penney?"

"Did you see something about her in the office?"

PC shook her head. "No, I didn't see anything about her there, but the two of them seem to be up to something."

"She may know more than she's telling, but when we first interviewed her, she said she'd been working overnight Friday. Her relief was scheduled to come in at seven in the morning but had car trouble and didn't arrive until nine. Daphne stopped for breakfast on the way home. We confirmed that with her employer and Winnie Hargraves at the City Café. Then she went home. Next-door neighbor's doorbell camera was triggered when her car pulled in. Didn't trigger again until she left for work at 10:30 Saturday night."

"I suppose it's theoretically possible for her to have slipped out the back, avoiding the camera, and made her way to the Biersal to meet up with Penney."

Tran shrugged. "Yeah, I guess. I think if she's involved, it's more likely that she helped Joaquin dispose of evidence or something like that."

"You're probably right."

Tran parked the car, and they made their way inside. PC got a cup of coffee and sat down in her makeshift conference room office. *May as well start with Thibodeaux.*

Racketeering, mail fraud, and wire fraud are all federal. *If he got life, wonder if he'd be willing to talk to us, if Tran and I paid him a visit?*

She made a search on the computer.

Looks like a model prisoner in FCI Bastrop. PC sighed with frustration. Thibodeaux had been paroled due to good behavior six months ago.

Maybe she'd get lucky if she googled him. She got a hit within seconds.

It was an obituary. Andre Thibodeaux had been fatally struck by a hit and run driver less than twenty-four hours after he got out of prison.

Guess you've gotta be careful what you wish for. On to the hospital.

Primary colors exploded off the screen as the cheerful web-page opened up. A digital assistant implored her to find a doctor and schedule an appointment now. She found a lot of information about the hospital, but none of it connected to Bradford Penney.

Next, she added Penney to the hospital query.

PC scanned down to the bottom of the results page. "Oh, no. How awful."

Chapter 11

THE SEARCH RESULT that had caught PC's attention was an article about an eight-year-old girl, Melissa Hirsch, and her mother, who had been killed by a speeding driver fleeing police. The driver had been apprehended, but there was no information about them. In the newspaper obituary, Steve Hirsch had requested that, in lieu of flowers, donations to the Bateman Children's Hospital, where the trauma team had fought valiantly to save Melissa, would be greatly appreciated.

How was Steve Hirsch related to Brad Penney? Penney's uncle, perhaps? Cousin? Is that why he was so fixated on the case? And why he donated money to the hospital?

PC checked her notes. The fatal accident happened a few days before Andre Thibodeaux was arrested. He was apprehended in a no-knock raid on his house, not involved in a chase.

Based on the date of the society page wedding announcement, Hirsch would probably have been mid-fifties at the time. Seems a bit late in life to have an 8-year-old, but it happens.

PC wondered if she had all the pieces. The more information she got, the less sure she was. She needed to dig deeper into Hirsch's background.

The detective searched online for articles with a Steve Hirsch byline. The last one he'd written for the Dallas paper was the one about Thibodeaux. PC tried several permutations of Steve Hirsch reporter, journalist, and writer. No luck. It was as if he'd dropped off the face of the Earth after that article.

The detective scowled at the screen. *I need more coffee before I start digging into the vital statistics records.*

"Hey, PC?" Tran stuck his head into the conference room.

"Yeah?"

"The results on that blood test are back."

"Now? I thought they'd be back Tuesday."

"Yeah, well. The cleaners unplugged the incubator to use the outlet for their vacuum, so he had to re-run it."

"And?"

Tran let out a breath. "Not human blood."

"Really. Is he sure?"

"Yeah. But he'll send it to Harris County Forensics if you ask him to."

"That probably won't be necessary. Did Joaquin ever show up?"

"Chief didn't want to confront him until the test results were back. We've been keeping an eye on him, though."

"And what's he been doing?"

"Mostly going back and forth to work."

PC shifted in her chair. "Why don't we go talk to him? Just because the blood on his shirt wasn't human doesn't mean he didn't kill Penney."

Joaquin Jones' car was in the parking lot. But the detective was beginning to wonder if he'd hitched a ride somewhere with friends until he finally answered on the seventh knock. "Who's there?" He yawned.

"Possumwood PD. We'd like to speak with you." Tran's voice was smooth as hot butter.

"About what?"

"We'd really prefer to come inside to do that, sir." PC said.

The door remained closed long enough that Tran turned to PC and opened his mouth to speak. Before he could, the security chain slid through its track and the deadbolt clicked open. Joaquin Jones stood in the doorway in nothing but a pair of baggy, flannel pajama pants.

"Fine. Come in."

They stepped into the apartment, and he closed the door behind them. Jones gestured to the sofa. "Can I get you a drink or anything?" He held eye contact with PC a little longer than was comfortable.

"No, thanks." PC sat down. She remembered when he'd approached her and Daisy in the parking lot of the *Silver Dollar Saloon* to caution them about looking too closely into the affairs of the owner and his business associate. *How deeply was Joaquin involved in these operations?*

Tran shook his head. "I'm good."

"Okay. What do you want?"

PC gestured toward the loveseat that was at right angles to the couch. "It would be a lot easier to talk if you sit down instead of standing behind us."

He plopped down in the chair and patted the seat beneath him. "I'm sitting."

"Thank you." PC leaned toward him. "Mr. Jones, we're really interested in hearing what you were up to last Saturday."

"You mean, how did I get blood on my shirt?"

"That, too," Tran replied.

Jones stretched his leg out to reach his phone, then started tapping on the screen. "I went out Saturday morning to run some errands. Had to go to Horice, and there was a coyote that had been hit on the side of the road. Didn't think much of it, but he moved as I drove past. Pulled over to check on him. He was hurt—at least one broken leg—but was trying to get up. I threw my hoodie over his head, picked him up, and put him in my car."

Jones showed them a picture he'd taken of the wounded song dog. His mouth was bloody. If the hoodie was over the canid's head, then it could have soaked up blood and transferred it to Jones' shirt.

"What time was this?" Tran uncrossed his legs.

"I don't know. 7:30? 8?"

PC nodded. "And then what happened?"

"I brought him back to the apartment. Tried to get Poncho to drink some water—"

"Poncho is the coyote?" PC asked.

Jones nodded. "Yeah. Had to call him something. He wouldn't drink. I came upstairs, looking for a wildlife place to take him. It took some time, but I finally found one north of Houston, so I drove him out there. Between the drive and the paperwork, it took up all of my morning. Was almost late for work."

PC adjusted her position, so she didn't slip off the edge of the couch. "What was the name of the place you left him?"

"Rewild Rehab. I can get you the receipt." Jones got up and left the living room.

When he returned, he handed a receipt for admission of one male coyote, HBC, to PC. Jones had donated $100 for his care.

She studied it for a few moments, trying to calculate drive times. Jones' story seemed plausible. "How is Poncho doing?"

Jones broke into a grin. "They think he's going to be alright, once his bones heal. I gave them the location where I found him, and once he's back on his feet, they'll release him there."

PC wondered if Poncho had family who missed him. She'd read somewhere that coyotes mated for life. She had a soft spot for the families of murdered fathers.

Tran looked at the ceiling for a moment. "Seems like a lot of effort to go through for a coyote."

Jones stiffened. "He needed help."

"I agree. You did a kind and generous thing for Poncho." PC smiled.

His shoulders relaxed a little. "I was just about to hop in the shower. Is there anything else you need from me?"

PC put her elbow on the arm of the sofa. "Well, I do have another question or two."

"Okay."

"How well did you know Bradford Penney?"

"Not very well." Joaquin drew a few circles in the air around his ear with an index finger. "He was kinda nutzo, if you ask me."

"Why do you say that?" Tran broke in.

"Last week—I think it was Thursday, but it might have been Wednesday—he came to the Dollar just after we opened at three. Wanted to speak with Mr. Braintree. Said he was looking for rats. Now, Mr. Braintree specifically said he doesn't talk to peddlers, and anyone who brought one into his office would be fired on the spot. So I told him we didn't need any pest control service."

I beg to differ. "What did he say?"

"He just laughed. Said he'd see Mr. Braintree around town and he'd take it up with him then. He left after that."

PC gave a little nod of understanding. "And that was the only interaction you had with Mr. Penney?"

Joaquin rubbed his eyes. "Yes."

"You're sure?"

"Why wouldn't I be?"

Tran leaned forward. "What did you get rid of?"

"Excuse me?"

The officer tapped his thumb on his own thigh. "You told your aunt that you got rid of something and wanted her advice."

Joaquin laughed softly. "Bruh... my mom is convinced that my apartment's haunted. I keep telling her that old plumbing makes weird noises, but she thinks I'm in danger. She sent me a big bundle of sage to burn to chase away the bad spirits. Tim, my roomie, started sneezing the second it came in the house. Obviously, I couldn't burn it, even if I wanted to. I can't just flat-out lie to my mom about burning the sage. Aunt Daphne was going to help me come up with a way to help Mom feel better about my living space without any wacky rituals."

The detective chuckled. "Well, that makes sense. What was the coyote's name again?"

"Poncho."

PC stood up. "I hope Poncho makes a full recovery. Thanks for your time."

Tran rose and followed her to the door.

They got in the car. PC let out a loud breath. "Wonder if he's lying."

Tran shifted into reverse. "About the coyote?"

"No. That seems true. About Penney. When I asked if he'd had any other interactions, he rubbed his eyes, then when I tried to get him to confirm, he answered my question with a question, instead of just saying 'yes.' Struck me as evasive. When I asked about the coyote, he answered without hesitation—he didn't have to think about the story."

"Or maybe he'd just woken up and had sleep in his eyes." Tran pulled into the street.

PC shrugged. "Possibly."

She stared out the window. The feed store had a plywood cut-out of the headless horseman, with a jack-o'-lantern perched on a little platform on the rider's raised hand. "What about Stacey Clemmons? If Penney was causing trouble by spreading lies about her and stalking around on her property, and she overheard the argument with Stan Zimmerman, she might have opted to solve her problem in a fermenting vat at the Biersal."

"I followed up—wasn't her. She was an hour and a half away with a dozen students and some of their parents, practicing at a horse show grounds. They left at 7:30 AM and didn't get back until almost 5:00 PM. Lots of people with her all day on Saturday."

After a mostly unproductive day of chasing wild geese with Tran, PC sat on the bed in her PJs, studying the black and white crime scene photos from her father's murder. She stared at the counter where his body had fallen. A display of candy was overturned, plastic-wrapped pecan pralines spilling across the Formica and onto the tile. Broken glass and eerily grey pickle juice glistened on the floor where the jar of jumbo dills had fallen. A few girthy gherkins lay scattered among the shards. A jar of pickled eggs had narrowly avoided the same fate. On the counter, a printed cardboard sign, asking for donations to a children's hospital, lay on its side.

Wait. How did I not notice this before?

Chapter 12

Trey Donovan had been a production engineer for an oil company before he and Rose opened the ShopStop. On a trip to the Middle East, he'd brought back an ornate antique box decorated with geometric patterns made from inlaid ebony wood and bone.

This box should have been attached to the sign requesting children's hospital donations. It was on neither the counter nor the floor. The person who robbed the ShopStop must have taken it away with the rest of the plunder. PC tapped the photo.

Had she seen it somewhere recently? Or just something similar?

A marble chess board?

The antique black and white checkerboard marble floor in Mayor Phineas Scott's house?

The Quenton Plantation Historical Site?

Drew's antique-loaded house?

The store, Vintage Glory Antiques?

Happily Ever Afters was a restored Victorian. They had no shortage of nineteenth-century items.

PC had been on the Azalea trail in the spring and toured several of the historic homes in town. *One of them, perhaps?*

Museum of Slovenian Culture?

None of those places seemed quite right. If she quit thinking about it, the answer would come to her. Probably at three in the morning. Or when she was driving and couldn't write anything down.

Saturday finally rolled around. PC and Drew waited in line for the ghost tour at the Afters. She surreptitiously searched her bag for the pack of cinnamon gum she knew was in there somewhere. The garlic breadsticks at *Zeno's Pizza* had been especially garlicky. It was delicious when she was eating it an hour earlier, but now the allium's scent was more fume than fragrance. She was afraid to talk to anyone, for fear of knocking them out with her anti-vampire breath.

Ah! Her fingers touched the thin cardboard, and she pulled it out of her bag. The detective took a stick for herself, then offered the pack to Drew. "Gum?"

"Yes, thank you." He slid a foil-wrapped stick out of the container.

He had also partaken of the garlic offerings. PC put the packet away and spotted a few folks she knew in the line of about twenty people.

She waved to Jim and Winnie Hargraves. The tour had been all they talked about on Wednesday night at darts.

Renetta Sherman, the real estate agent, turned her head away when PC looked in her direction.

Omar Schmidt raised his arm over his head and waved at them. The detective guessed business at the Dollarmore was going well—he looked happy. Drew gave him a low wave.

Near the end of the line stood Hunter Braintree with a questionably young woman on one arm and an unlit cigar in his opposite hand. He grinned at PC. She nodded back.

The front doors clicked and opened wide. A woman in a Victorian black mourning dress stepped onto the veranda. She carried a small lantern lit by a candle. Scalloped black lace edged the square neckline, showcasing an ivory cameo on a short silver chain that rested just below her throat. On her close-fitting jacket, a silk front placket with braided frog closures was framed by a column of jet beads in the seam line that became beaded fringe along the hem. More beads and lace dripped from the cuffs. *Is that Simone Reynolds underneath the thick veil?*

"Welcome to the *Happily Ever Afters'* fall tours. Some guests have experienced some discomfort in the house, so please notify your guide if at any time you don't feel you are able to continue. You will be walking up one flight of stairs. If you are unable to do so, we do have an elevator for those with mobility issues. Be very careful to stay with your guide. And remember, this is a candlelight tour. The rooms are illuminated just like they would have been in the nineteenth century, but the hallways may be dark. Please come in."

The tour-takers filed through into the front parlor. Wall sconces bore flickering candles, and a fire crackled in the fireplace.

Once Simone shut the door, Dinah Mae Brown, the president of the Mirabella County Historical Society, appeared in the doorway, dressed in sky-blue silk and carrying a candle enclosed in a glass lantern. PC assumed it was to reduce the fire hazard and keep candlewax from dripping everywhere.

Dinah Mae raised the light and shone it on the assembled crowd. "Tonight, we will step back into the year 1880, when Thomas Brenderman's mansion was completed and he and his bride, Eliza Marberger Brenderman, moved in. Follow me."

She led the way into the ballroom. Multiple crystal chandeliers dangled from the ceiling and eight-foot-tall candelabras holding twenty candles each stood like rigid soldiers around the room. Even so, the light was not bright, and shadows danced in the far corners. Red velvet sofas lined the walls.

The ballroom had looked so different when they'd had the Valentine's brunch there back in February. Tables and serving stations had covered the fancy parquet floor, and it had been brightly lit by sunlight shining through large, east-facing picture windows. This evening really *did* feel like a step back in time.

A string quartet burst into a waltz, and PC jumped, bumping into Drew. "Sorry."

In the dim light, she'd assumed the group seated against the back wall was a bunch of decorative mannequins, like the ones at the Quenton Plantation. A couple, elegantly dressed in Victorian attire, swept in from the conservatory and swirled around the ballroom in three-quarter time.

As they danced, Dinah Mae spoke. "Thomas and Eliza were fond of throwing lavish parties that lasted the entire weekend, from Friday afternoon to Sunday afternoon. Thomas had attended Baylor College, back when it was still in Independence, with Sam Houston's youngest son, Temple Lea Houston. It's possible that Thomas and Temple met on a riverboat as young teenagers, but that has yet to be verified. Temple was a frequent guest at the Brenderman house until he was appointed district attorney in the Panhandle in 1882."

The music finished, and the couple bowed to each other.

"A popular dance in this era was the German Cotillion, or the German. It's the grandmother of modern square dancing. As guests of Thomas and Eliza, you will be participating in this dance. Ladies, please line up behind Eliza, gentlemen behind Thomas."

PC's mouth fell open. "I…"

Drew took her arm and led her out to the waiting couple. "It's a different dance every year. Last time, it was the polka. Just do what Eliza does." He parked her in the ladies' line and stepped over to the gents'.

Even though he was only six feet away, it felt like six miles. Jim and Winnie had talked about dancing, but there was no indication of audience participation. If PC had known she was expected to caper about the ballroom, she probably wouldn't have come. She was good at many things. Dancing was not one of them. She looked over her shoulder, wondering if she could slink out the back door.

Winnie Hargraves got in line right behind PC. "Hey, sugar! How's your mama?"

"She's good, thanks."

"Good. You give Rose a hug for me when you get home. This is so excitin'. We do this every year. Jim pulled a hamstring doing the polka last time, though. I told him he shouldn't have overdone those kicks."

PC smiled at the thought of Jim Hargraves, who was only a couple of years younger than Rose, leaping like Mikhail Baryshnikov on this very floor. It was exactly the sort of thing Jim would do. He was all about wearing out rather than rusting away, and Winnie was right there with him. Probably why the detective liked the Hargraves so much.

There were more women than men on the tour, so Dinah Mae assigned two of them to the men's line.

She counted heads again, then nodded. "There were many patterns that might have been danced with the German, and things could get... very lively. We're going to learn one simple pattern this evening. Follow your leader and have fun. It's a party, remember?"

A simple pattern. I can do a simple pattern.

The quartet began to play. Eliza and Thomas faced each other, side-by-side, raised their right hands to eye level, and pressed them together, palms flat. She held her left arm out and he folded his behind his back. They walked in a circle, stopping every two steps to stretch one leg at a time out in front and tap their toes on the floor. The other dancers followed their example.

Drew's eyes stayed locked on PC's.

This isn't so bad. I can do this.

She smiled to her partner. Victorian dancing hadn't been on her bucket list, but it wasn't nearly as bad as she had imagined. It may not have crossed the line into 'fun,' but she was enjoying it.

The lines re-formed. Then Eliza turned to the man next to Thomas. Everyone crisscrossed and repeated the step with a new partner. Jim Hargraves was a pretty good dancer. Which was good for PC—she had less rhythm than a wounded bird.

So far, so good.

This pattern was repeated twice more, and PC was now on her fifth dance partner.

"Hey, Sis."

"Mr. Braintree."

His hand pressed against hers more like he was trying to arm wrestle her than dance. She dropped her hand quickly and his arm flopped forward. PC put her hand up again, and he gave her a smarmy smile as he placed his palm against hers.

"How's your investigation coming?"

"Ongoing."

He stopped to tap his toes on the floor before PC did, and she almost got an elbow to the face.

"Joaquin's a good kid. You need to quit harassing him."

The detective shrugged. "We just follow the trail of the evidence."

Braintree snorted. "That twig? Do you really think he brained the newspaper guy with a crowbar and lifted him up into that tank?"

The circle was completed, and PC happily left the truculent Braintree to return to her place in line. After struggling all week with zero progress, she'd wanted a break from the intransigent case. Now Braintree had brought it back into sharp focus, and she was already struggling to keep up with the dance steps.

PC prepared to crisscross again, but now Eliza directed the women's group to hold hands and form a big circle. Thomas did the same with the men, except they surrounded the ladies and didn't hold hands. The men began to skip in a clockwise direction. The ladies also started skipping in a circle. Unfortunately for PC, they were going counterclockwise, and she had been following the men. The detective nearly knocked over a petite young woman with light blue hair.

"I'm so sorry!"

"It's fine," the other woman muttered as she tried to catch up with the galloping ladies.

Finally, they moved back into lines, but the ladies and men were at opposite ends from their original partners. They danced with the remaining five people, then the music stopped. Eliza stepped into the space between the lines and curtsied. Thomas did the same but bowed to her. The tour-takers just bowed or curtsied to their current partners.

Dinah Mae snatched back control. "Now, during an evening of dancing, the hosts would have provided plenty of refreshments."

Simone appeared at the entrance to the conservatory, holding open the door and beckoning. The group flowed into the glassed-in room. Condensation from the warm, moist evening dripped down the panes outside. A buffet set with finger foods filled the room with mouth-watering aromas.

PC read the labels in front of each offering: tiny apple pies, scones with beauty berry jelly and clotted cream, venison meatballs, persimmon tarts, and wild turkey croquettes. A crystal punch bowl held steaming mulled apple cider. Notes of cinnamon, cloves, and cardamom danced above the sweet and tangy aroma of hot apple juice. It certainly smelled like fall inside, even if it didn't feel like it outside.

After fifteen minutes or so of snacking and chatting, Dinah Mae rang a brass hand bell that sat on the edge of the buffet.

"We will be continuing our tour in five minutes. Now is a good time to avail yourself of the facilities, should you so require, before we go upstairs. If anyone needs assistance with the stairs, please come and see me now."

Drew wiped his mouth and PC drank the last of her cider.

He proffered his elbow. "What do you think so far?"

She took his arm. "Honestly, I thought we were just going to walk around the house with either Simone or Caitlyn telling us about 1800s celebrities who either slept here or waved from their carriages as the horses trotted by. I wasn't expecting all this." She gestured from the buffet to the punch station.

He grinned and his mouth opened.

The brass bell rang again.

"Ladies and gentlemen, let us proceed upstairs."

Chapter 13

THE CENTURY-AND-A-HALF-YEAR-OLD STAIRCASE creaked under the group's feet. The dark wood was firm and steady, from the intricately carved bannisters to the well-worn stair treads.

Landscapes and a portrait of a collie decorated the velvet damask wallpaper on the landing where the stairway made a 90° turn. PC thought she could make out the initials 'EB.' Had Eliza Brenderman painted these?

At the top of the staircase, the tour group pooled in the small sitting area.

Dinah Mae cleared her throat and gestured to a large photograph facing the stairs. "This is the Brenderman family in 1888. The photo was processed usin' the gelatin silver method, one of the new processes using a paper backin', rather than glass or metal plates."

Thomas Brenderman sat in a delicate Queen Anne chair, the sepia and silvery-grey tones of the photo making his light-colored eyes uncanny in his angular face. Eliza stood beside him, a swaddled baby in one arm and a tearful toddler on her hip. Three young children—two girls and a boy—stood in front of her. The tallest, a boy of six or seven, held the reins of a shaggy pinto pony, most of which was out of frame.

"The boy holdin' the pony is Thomas Zebulon Brenderman, Junior. He was called 'Tom,' to distinguish him from his father, and sadly, young Tom fell down the stairs and died not long after this portrait was taken. Guests have reported hearin' a child laughin' and the sound of a ball bouncin' in the hallways at night."

PC leaned toward Drew. "Probably squirrels in the attic."

He quirked an eyebrow.

After surveying the group, Dinah Mae continued. "Thomas and Eliza's youngest son, Abner—the baby—never returned from Belleau Wood during World War I. The story goes that one mornin' Eliza was in her bedroom on the third floor and saw him comin' up the walk in his uniform, carryin' a rifle and a pack on his back. He was almost to the house, and she ran down the stairs to meet him. Eliza flung open the door to find him standin' on the mat. But when she tried to throw her arms around his neck, he vanished. Eliza was so distraught she took to her bed for the rest of the day. A few weeks later, she received a telegram from the Marine Corps informin' her that Abner had died in the line of duty. When she saw the date of his death was the same as the day she had seen him, she fainted dead away. Eliza never fully recovered from this experience."

Dinah Mae raised her lantern aloft and glided from the sitting area, across the hall, and into the upstairs parlor.

Three women sat in the armchairs, dressed in the fashion of upper crust Victorians. One wore a bluish green dress, another a gold dress with black polka dots and black-striped sleeves, and the third wore a white and purple-polka-dotted bodice and overskirt over a ruffled purple skirt. The woman in gold and black read a book, while the other two played a game of cards.

A narrow box, approximately one foot long and four inches wide, sat on a low table between the green and purple ladies. The top of the box was divided into three rows of inlaid woods and ivory. The middle row was a herringbone pattern of medium and dark woods, with a plain square with a small hole in it at each end. The top and bottom rows consisted of what looked like skinny dominoes, each ivory 'domino' separated by inlaid wood stripes.

Wooden pegs, some dark, some light, stuck out of the holes in the 'dominoes.' A pile of cards lay in front of the box.

"Ha!" cried Ms. Violet. "A triplet." She laid the Jack of Hearts on the pile and moved a dark peg.

Dinah Mae faced the tour group. "Cribbage was a very popular Victorian parlor game. These ladies are entertainin' themselves while their husbands are in the billiard room, drinkin' whiskey and possibly smokin' cigars, if any are available. Eliza's mother, Rachel Lamartine Marberger, moved in after the death of her husband, Heinze. She spent much of her time in this room, as the light was particularly good. Rachel was an avid reader and aspirin' novelist. She had a short story published in the Houston Post under the pen name of Frank Martin, but never completed her long form manuscript. On nights when the moon is bright, visitors have reported hearing a rhythmic scratchin' sound, as if someone were writin' with a fountain pen. The drawers of Rachel's writin' desk are frequently found open."

PC studied the escritoire. "The floor probably sags just a little bit in the middle, or the foundation's shifted. Gravity, not ghosts."

Drew rubbed his forehead.

Dinah Mae led the group past the relaxing women and into the next room. Floor-to-ceiling bookshelves were crammed full of books, some lying horizontally on top of their vertical peers for lack of space. A thick Persian rug covered most of the wood floor, from the wall to the door that opened to the hallway. Near the window, a mahogany table stood at one end of the rug. A four-taper candelabra flickered near a young man who sat with a book opened on the table. He took notes with a thick silver and blue pen. A pair of dark leather armchairs, with a small round table between them, took up the other end.

"Robert Martin Brenderman inherited the estate when Thomas passed. He was a student of philosophy when he wasn't runnin' the family businesses. The Brendermans owned a flour mill and had purchased the local cotton gin from its original owner, Heinrich Mueller, for a bargain basement price. With the official openin' of the Port of Houston in 1914, Robert established an import/export business that made him an even wealthier man. Still, his most prized possession was an original copy of Immanuel Kant's *Metaphysics of Morals*. The owners of *Happily Ever Afters* sent that book to the Quenton Plantation Historical Site for preservation by professional archivists. The owners attempted to replace it with a modern printing but found it lyin' on the floor every mornin'. After they removed the offendin' book, no further activity has been reported."

Drew looked to PC, eyebrows raised in expectation of her logical explanation.

"You see how packed these shelves are. It probably didn't fit all the way in. If the foundation's shifted, it would be shifted for this room too, not just the parlor."

He chuckled quietly.

"What?"

He looked away and shook his head.

Dinah Mae's lantern rose into the air, and she made her way to the door that exited into the hallway. "Watch your step, please. The corridor can be a mite gloomy."

A shadow moved along the wall. *Was that... a man? No. Must be the flickering candlelight. Or was it one of the role players alerting the next group that we're coming.*

Yellow light spilled from an open doorway across the hall from the library. The clack of ivory balls striking each other, and then rolling away was unmistakable. Dinah Mae led them into the billiards room.

Four gentlemen in waistcoats stood around a bulky furnishing half again as long as a modern pool table. Elaborately carved wood framed the green felt-covered playing surface. The eight fat, carved legs looked more like decorative urns than furniture parts. A man with a handlebar mustache leaned over the table and lined up his cue. A green ball rolled to the edge of the hole, but didn't go in. The other men laughed, and the shooter took a sip of an amber drink.

"Billiards was popular among the men of Thomas Brenderman's time. After dinner, they retired to the billiard room to drink, smoke, and discuss subjects that were not considered appropriate to talk about in front of the ladies. While smokin' is not allowed here at *Happily Ever Afters*, Thomas and his companions might have smoked pipes, cigars, or the increasin'ly popular cigarettes. Sadly, he dropped dead from a massive heart attack in this very room in 1910. Guests have complained of the smell of cigar smoke here, and the hallway near the door. One man reported being tapped on the shoulder as he lined up his shot."

The tour-takers murmured.

"Almost until the day she died, Eliza used to come sit in here and talk to her dead husband. It was never clear if she really believed she could see him, or if she just needed to talk out her day. However, it is documented that she had trouble keepin' maids. One young lady was fired for gossipin' about Eliza, saying she smoked cigars, which would have been unthinkable for a lady in the early 1900s. Now some folks believe that if you hold on too tight to your loved ones after they pass, they can't cross over to the other side. That's why the restless spirit of Thomas Brenderman may be trapped in this room, stogie and all."

At the back of the group, PC leaned over to Drew. "It's drafty up here. Probably someone smoking outside. Smoke came in through the cracks."

"You don't have to try so hard to debunk everything. What are you, Harry Houdini?" Drew whispered.

"What does an escape artist have to do with it?"

"Most people know Erik Weisz, a.k.a. Harry Houdini, as an escapologist, and that's true. But he was also famous for debunking seances and psychics. After his mother died, he was desperate to confirm that there was some form of life after death. His close friend, Sir Arthur Conan Doyle, took him to visit a purported medium. She gave him fifteen pages of messages. Problem was, they were all in English, and Mrs. Weisz only spoke Hungarian. This made Houdini so angry that not only did it ruin his friendship with Doyle, but set him on the warpath, vowing to expose fakes and charlatans of all stripes, but especially Spiritualists." Drew bit his lip. "I'm giving you another TED Talk, aren't I?"

"It's one of your best qualities." PC gave him a lopsided-grin. "I always thought Houdini was Italian."

"He took his stage name from the French magician, Jean-Eugène Robert-Houdin. He just added an 'i' on the end of Houdin. Lots of performers take stage names, but he did this as a matter of personal safety—his father was a rabbi, and, sadly, there was a rising tide of antisemitism during his lifetime."

A woman turned around and glared at them.

PC sighed and shook her head.

Dinah Mae's lantern rose above the tour-takers. "Let us adjourn to the sewin' room."

The group followed her back into the hallway and toward the stairs. She entered the next room, and the guests flowed in behind her.

A black and gold Singer manual sewing machine was bolted to a small table underneath a wall sconce opposite the door. Wheels on the machine and side of the table were connected by a thin rubber belt, and there were what looked a great deal like bicycle pedals attached to rods that ran from one side of the machine to the other, just inches from the floor.

Three ladies sat in a group, distributed over a sofa and a chaise lounge.

Dinah Mae gestured toward the Singer. "Eliza Brenderman was lucky enough to have received a sewin' machine as a weddin' present. While all of her dresses were made and tailored by a professional seamstress, Eliza greatly enjoyed usin' her machine for quiltin'. Her maid was allowed access to repair items for the family and to sew her own clothes."

The three historical role players tittered.

"Eliza's sisters, Pearl and Amanda, and her cousin Sarah were frequent guests at the Brenderman household, and they often brought their needlework as they visited in the sewin' room. Amanda, in the blue, was known for her tattin'. If you're not familiar, it's a kind of lace made with a shuttle or a needle."

The role-player in blue slid an oblong white object, pointed at the ends, and about the size of a pack of gum, along a piece of string. On one end was a spool, and on the other was a band of lace formed of interconnecting loops and circles.

"Now Sarah was not quite as well off as her cousins, and she had what y'all might call a side hustle of teachin' embroidery to the girls in the town."

The woman in pink leaned forward, displaying the hoop holding the sampler she was working on. 3-D silk ribbon flowers bloomed above green spring bushes made of mixed colors of thread.

"Pearl sold the ornate doilies she made. It was her version of egg money. Even though her husband gave her an allowance, he demanded a strict accountin' of her spendin'. The doily money was her walkin' around cash."

The green lady held a circle of lace in her left hand, while a thin, cream-colored crochet hook in her right flashed in and out of the white cotton, adding to the doily one rapid, fine stitch at a time.

"Guests have been awakened by the clickin' of the treadle, that's the bottom part you work with your feet, and the clackin' of the needle goin' up and down. The owners used to leave a piece of sample fabric in there for display, but somebody kept sewin' on it and usin' up the thread."

PC crossed her arms. "I'm sure it was just the guests."

Dinah Mae raised her light. "This is the last room on the tour. We're gonna head back down the stairs now. Watch your step, please."

When they returned to the ballroom, Simone was there to give them each a small swag bag. Dinah Mae thanked the tour-takers for coming and passed a hat for donations to the Historical Society.

The visitors were slow to depart, clumping into groups and chatting.

The historian clapped her hands. "Could I get y'all to move your visitin' outside? There's another tour at 8:30."

PC's phone vibrated. She glanced at it to make sure it wasn't Rose or Daisy.

It was Tran. "Just a heads up. Zimmerman's alibi just fell apart."

Chapter 14

"WHAT?" PC SAID out loud, blinking at the text message.

"What's wrong?" Drew guided her through the slowly dispersing group of tour-takers on their way to the parking lot.

"Message from Tran. He says Ken Zimmerman's alibi just blew up."

"I can't believe he'd have anything to do with the murder."

"Me, either."

Drew unlocked the car and opened the door for PC. "Does this mean you want to bail on coffee?"

"Of course not! I'll just ask what happened on the way to Jillibella's."

She responded to the text with three question marks.

Her phone rang in answer.

"So, what happened?"

"Good evening to you, too."

"Sorry. We just finished up the ghost tour and we're in the car."

"Got it. Ken said he left the Biersal between 7 and 7:30, right?"

"Yeah."

"So that would have put him in Houston between 8 and 8:30."

"Yeah."

"On Saturday morning about 7:45, an 18-wheeler tanker truck jackknifed on the Katy Freeway just past the 610 Loop. They shut everything down for a hazmat team to clean up the spill. The freeway was closed for four hours. No way for him to have checked in to his hotel in New Orleans at 2:00 if he left when he said he did."

PC knew the area well. That part of I-10 ran along the bottom of a concrete spaghetti bowl of curling freeway intersections. Any accident there would be difficult to clear because it was sandwiched by overpasses on either side. "So, he had to have left an hour earlier than he said. But didn't Dr. Mack say the time of death was between 8 and 4?"

"He also said it could have been earlier or later. Because the body was in the cold fermentation tank, it was hard to tell. Ken lied about when he left—he's hiding something."

"Have you talked to him yet?"

Tran's phone crackled, as if he'd dropped it. "Sorry about that. No, trying to locate him."

"Well. Keep me posted."

"Will do."

The detective put away her phone.

Drew pulled into a parking space at the TexMex restaurant. "I gather Ken got the time he left wrong?"

"Yeah." PC almost wished Tran hadn't messaged her. After a tough week, she just wanted a night off to relax and have fun. Was that too much to ask? Retirement had made her less tolerant of the common hazards of a j-o-b.

Before long, they were seated opposite each other at a small table in the back of the restaurant, a pot of decaf between them.

Drew stirred creamer into his coffee. "So, what did you think of the tour?"

"It was good. Never done anything like that before. I know how much Dinah Mae likes her historical re-enactors, so that didn't surprise me. But I was not at all expecting the dancing part."

"Did you like it?"

"Well." PC sipped her coffee. "It was fun to do once. Not sure I'd want to do it every weekend." *Or again.*

He chuckled. "Yeah. They go all out. Wait 'til you see their Christmas decorations."

"I'd heard they… are enthusiastic."

Their server arrived with a large plate. "Your sopapillas."

She placed the serving dish of puffy little golden-brown pillows of fried dough, sprinkled in cinnamon and drizzled with honey, in the center of the table, then supplied each of them with their own small plate.

"Thank you." PC reached for one. "I didn't think I was hungry until I smelled these." She dropped the sopapilla on her plate and shook her hand. "Fresh out of the fryer."

Drew used a fork to scoop a couple onto his plate. "I'll let mine cool a little."

PC unrolled her silverware from the napkin and speared one of the sweet treats. She considered it for some time.

"Whatcha thinking?"

She waved her fork back and forth. "I almost wish you hadn't told me about Harry Houdini. I'd gone my entire life thinking he was a happy Italian guy. And it turns out he had to change his name to hide his identity to stay safe."

"I'm sorry."

The detective shrugged. "Usually when people change their names, it's because they're trying to hide from past mistakes." She tentatively took a bite of the sopapilla.

"How is it?"

"Mmmm." PC swallowed. "Really good."

They leisurely drank coffee and ate sopapillas while they talked about the ghost tour, the Afters, the upcoming Halloween Ball, and Tran and Annie's fast-approaching wedding. It wasn't until they noticed they were the last ones in the restaurant that they left.

PC had just gotten out of the shower and gone back to her room to dress when the text chime on her phone chirped.

"You coming in soon?"

Why was Tran messaging her so early? "Yes. Why?"

"Just got the report back on the crowbar."

"And?"

"Come see."

She slipped into her customary khakis and polo shirt. She'd already blotted her short hair in the bathroom, so she quickly finger-combed it on her way out the door.

"Mama? You got everything you need? I'm going to work."

"I'm not an invalid, Primrose. Terry's pickin' me up for lunch after while and we're goin' to the Red Brangus in Horice."

"Have fun."

At the station, Annie buzzed PC into the secure area, and she headed straight for Tran's cube. He sat at his desk, tapping on the computer keyboard.

PC stopped right behind him, looking over his shoulder. "Now. What about the crowbar?"

"It was rusty."

"We already knew that."

"But there were also traces of blood. Too early to get the DNA results back, but the blood type is O negative. Same as Bradford Penney."

The detective whistled. "O negative? That's rare."

"Exactly."

"Have you scheduled Ken Zimmerman for a second interview?"

"He should be coming in any minute now."

Tran's cell buzzed and he picked it up. "Okay. I'll come get him." He disconnected. "Speak of the devil. He's here now."

PC followed Tran down the hall to retrieve their suspect. *Why did he lie? Would they get the truth this time?*

Tran pulled open the security door. "Mr. Zimmerman?"

Ken, looking a few shades paler than usual, stepped inside. Little beads of sweat dotted his hairline.

"Thank you for coming in. We just needed to clarify a few things. Come with me."

Zimmerman followed Tran and PC followed Zimmerman to the interrogation room. He opened the door and gestured inside. Zimmerman stepped inside as if he thought a giant rat trap was about to snap shut on him. PC entered the tiny room as well.

Tran smiled at his suspect. "Would you like anything to drink? Water? A coke?"

Zimmerman swallowed noticeably. "I guess a coke would be good. You have Sprite?"

"I think so." Tran left.

PC sat closer to Zimmerman than she needed to, her knees almost touching his, invading his space. Although in fairness, she couldn't have gotten much further away. The room was not much bigger than a closet.

"How've you been, Ken?"

"This has been hard. Not gonna lie."

"I understand. How's Stan holding up? He's the one who led the tour straight into the unfortunate Mr. Penney."

"He's a mess. Marlene took him into Houston yesterday to see a shrink."

PC nodded. "That's good. A therapist can really help."

Seeing the aftermath of a murder was a slow trauma that built up over time. No matter how many defenses you put up, sooner or later, there would always be a case that broke you. For someone who wasn't expecting to come upon a body? That would leave a mark.

Zimmerman rubbed his forehead. "Yeah. Maybe."

Tran came back with a bottle of 7-Up. "Hope this is okay."

The subject nodded. Tran closed the door and stood next to it.

PC let Zimmerman take a swig of his drink. "What time did you say you left for New Orleans?"

He coughed and almost spat out his soda. "I don't know. 7, 7:30. Something like that."

"And you took 720 to FM 999 to I-10?"

"Well, yeah. What other way would I go?"

"And how long does it typically take to get to Houston from here?"

"Little over an hour."

The detective leaned forward. "Ken, an 18-wheeler jack-knifed on I-10 and the Loop at 7:45. The road was shut down for four hours."

He bowed his head.

"What time did you really leave?" Tran asked.

Zimmerman covered his face with his hands.

"Ken?" PC bumped his leg with hers.

His head remained down. "You have to swear not to tell my wife."

Oh, Ken. What have you done?

"We're listening."

"I have diabetes," he announced.

"Sorry to hear that," PC said.

"I can't go to New Orleans without stopping at *Café DuMonde* for beignets. Do you have any idea what fried white flour and powdered sugar do to your glucose?"

"Don't you have insulin?" Tran's voice dripped with incredulity.

"I didn't bring it with me. Didn't go back to the house."

I can understand why you wouldn't want your wife to know.

"That was part of the reason I slept so hard at the hotel."

Tran cleared his throat. "You lied to the police because you were afraid to tell your wife you stopped for donuts?"

"Beignets! Not the same thing. And I didn't exactly lie… so much as I got the time wrong."

PC broke in. "Ken, do you own a crowbar?"

"A crowbar?"

"Yes. Do you own one?"

He looked at her quizzically. "Not sure. Probably."

The detective stood up. "I think that's all I had. Do you have any more questions, Tran?"

"No, I don't think so. Thank you for stopping by, Mr. Zimmerman. I'll show you out."

PC walked down the corridor to her ad hoc office in the conference room while Tran escorted Zimmerman to the lobby. He came in a minute later and leaned on the table.

"Well? What do you think?"

"He didn't react the way I would have expected if he'd bashed Penney with the crowbar. I don't think he did it."

Tran ran his tongue over his teeth. "I agree with you. Now what?"

"I think we're back to our only other good suspect, Joaquin Jones. Yes, the blood on his shirt was coyote blood, but there is the matter of the cocktail sword found near the body. That's got to be something a bartender could easily slip into his pocket without thinking or drop into his shoe by mistake."

"The Biersal doesn't use those?"

"They don't serve mixed drinks. Beer only."

Tran frowned. "I guess I'll call the wildlife rescue and check on Poncho. They can confirm the time Joaquin arrived."

PC scoured notes and witness statements, looking for inconsistencies. After a while, her stomach rumbled, and she looked at her FlitBit. It was well past lunchtime. Tran had gone out to run some calls. She'd just pop home for a quick bite.

A package leaned against the front door when she arrived at Rose's house. PC picked it up and brought it inside. Terry and Rose sat on the couch, holding hands and watching TV.

"This came for you, Mama." PC smiled at Terry. "How was your lunch?"

He grinned back at her. "Good."

Rose got up and hurried to the kitchen to retrieve a knife. She cut the tape, pulled open the flaps, and rummaged around in the packing material.

"Here we go." She opened the plastic envelope. "Now, I got this for Cordite. The weather's gettin' cold, and I thought he needed a little somethin'. I had to get him the junior size. Hope it fits."

He hasn't needed a coat yet, but okay.

Plastic crinkled as the item came out of the package. Rose unsnapped the closure and pulled out what appeared to be a miniature horse blanket. It was quilted, and possibly waterproof. PC coughed to cover her gasp of surprise at the purple paisley print. Amoebas, highlighted in green, yellow, and teal, squirmed across a gradient purple background. Was it horrifying… or brilliant?

"Mama, that sure looks… warm. Come here, Cordie. Let's try on your new outfit."

The dog slunk over to her, his eyes down as if he were embarrassed. PC put his head through the opening, then adjusted the straps. Seemed to be a good fit. He might be happy to have the peculiar paisley for cold and rainy walks.

Cordite jumped onto the couch and searched Rose's face with beseeching eyes.

PC snickered. But another look at the dog coat made her stop.

Wait. I know who the killer is. But I'm not sure I can prove it.

Chapter 15

PC SAT IN Tran's personal car in the parking lot of the *Best Southern Motel*, adjusting a pendant that contained a tiny microphone. Woody tapped on the window, and she rolled it down.

"You sure about this, Donovan?"

"Yeah. Without a confession, there isn't enough hard evidence for the DA to work with."

"You aren't wrong. But he's dangerous. This could go sideways in a hurry."

"I know. If I need an extraction, I'll say, 'That dog won't hunt,' okay?"

"Tran or Gorman should be doing this."

"Yeah, but Braintree won't talk to them, though. He thinks he can lord it over the 'little lady,' and nothing will happen because he's too big and bad to be taken down by a girl. But you know what? Dollars to donuts the *Silver Dollar Saloon* is at the epicenter of the local crime wave."

Woody sighed and PC rolled the window back up. She started opening the door and had to wait for him to move out of the way. She took a deep breath, smiled, and headed for the entrance to the Best Southern.

A bell clanked dully as she entered the lobby, as if it had given up any sparkle it might once have had to hang on the grimy door of the no-tell motel. Immediately in front of her was the shabby alcove, where morning continental breakfast was served, and a couple of vending machines squatted. To her right, the greasy front desk clerk sat behind bullet-proof glass, scrolling through his phone.

On her left was the dark cavern of the *Silver Dollar Saloon*. There were no windows, so the lurid neon beer signs and the sallow recessed bulbs provided the only lighting.

She glanced down to make sure her necklace was facing the right way and stepped into the dingy bar.

Joaquin Jones dried a glass with a white towel. He crooked an eyebrow. "Is there something I can get for you, Detective?"

"Do you have orange juice? In a bottle?"

He eyed her for a long moment, then turned to a refrigerated case behind the bar. He moved some cans of soda around and produced a small carton. PC took it, surprised it was actual juice, and not orange-flavored beverage.

"So, um, how's Poncho?"

"Did you come here to ask about the coyote?"

"Not specifically..."

"They were able to fix his legs. He's going to be fine."

PC unscrewed the top of the juice box. "Good. I'm glad to hear that. Is Mr. Braintree in his office?"

"Why?"

"I'd like to talk to him for a minute."

"I'll ask if he's available."

Joaquin reached for a phone underneath the counter and pressed a button. "Mr. Braintree? Detective Donovan is here to see you... okay."

"He'll be out in a minute."

PC chugged her juice, her throat drier than it should have been.

After a few minutes, Braintree strode down the narrow hallway into the bar, a wide grin on his face. "Hey, Sis."

"Mr. Braintree. You sure you don't want to talk in your office?"

"I'm sure."

The detective glanced at Joaquin before gesturing toward the downtrodden belly of the bar. "Okay. Let's sit down and talk."

Braintree clapped her on the shoulder and led her to a table in the corner of the bar. He even pulled out a chair for her. Under other circumstances, she would have rejected his choice and insisted on a different seat, one she pulled out herself.

"Alright, Sis. What's on your mind?"

"Were you the driver?"

The big man tilted his head. "Come again?"

"Did you intentionally hit Devon and Melissa Hirsch, a mother and her young daughter, leaving them to die, out of revenge against Steve Hirsch's investigative reporting on your boss's syndicate? Or was it an accident?"

Braintree leaned back in his chair. "Why are you asking me that, Sis?"

"The last article Steve Hirsch wrote was about Andre Thibodeaux. After his family died, he disappeared like a ghost."

"And?"

"How soon did you recognize Bradford Penney as Steve Hirsch?"

The unctuous grin was back. "I never forget a face, Sis. First time I saw him, I knew who he was. But what of it?"

"He didn't get in that fermenting vat by himself."

Braintree shrugged. "Probably not, but why do you think I had anything to do with it?"

"We found a green plastic cocktail sword near the body. Something that would come from a bar. Pointed to Joaquin, at first, given that he had been acting very suspiciously."

The bartender made a show of polishing the bar.

"Later, when we were in Penney's office, there was a newspaper clipping from a 1950s society page about Paisley Penney and Stephen Hirsch tying the knot. There were also a couple of old photos of someone I assumed to be Brad Penney and his wife and child. And I wasn't exactly wrong about that. After we found that Mr. Penney had made monthly donations to the Bateman Children's Hospital, we discovered that Steve Hirsch had a daughter who was treated there around the same time as he wrote that article about Thibodeaux. He went to jail because you turned state's evidence, didn't he?"

"Doesn't prove I did anything. Why would I kill anybody?"

"Mr. Braintree, you know the answer to that question as well as I do."

Braintree's eyes narrowed, but he said nothing.

"I thought that Brad Penney and Steve Hirsch were probably cousins or related in some other way. That was until Mama got a sweater for my dog."

Braintree sent a facsimile of a smile. "And what does a dog sweater have to do with anything?"

"Glad you asked. You see, first she said she needed a junior size. Then when she pulled it out of the box, it was an astonishing purple paisley. That's when it hit me. The hospice nurse had told me that Bradford Penney's mother's name was Paisley. She was married to Stephen Bradford Hirsch. Senior. Their son was Steve Hirsch, junior, the journalist, who seemed to have dropped off the face of the earth after the murder of his family."

"Murder is a strong word. Can you prove that?"

"I only have to prove this one. When we looked into Bradford Penney's employment history, he started working for the newspaper in San Antonio six months after Steve Hirsch disappeared. But he didn't disappear. He reinvented himself under the protection of a new name. Just like Harry Houdini. Ten years ago, Steve Hirsch's widowed mother, Paisley Penney Hirsch moved in with him. He'd taken his father's middle name and his mother's maiden name to become Bradford Penney."

"People change their names all the time. Nothing to do with me."

"Interesting you should mention that. We found a note in his office that referenced a rat hunter. Given that he had accused the Zimmermans of harboring rats at the Biersal, we assumed that's what it was about. But that was completely wrong. He was talking about you, Hunter the Rat."

Braintree's head tilted down and his eyebrows tilted up. "Me?"

"Yes. You know where you made your biggest mistake?"

He scoffed and looked away.

"When we danced at the Afters, and you tried to defend Joaquin. How did you know that Penney had been hit with a crowbar?"

"It was on the news.

"No. Blunt force trauma wasn't confirmed until the autopsy, and the crowbar wasn't found until later, so the initial news report wouldn't have mentioned either one. Everyone who was there saw him in the fermentation tank, but only the killer would know he'd been knocked out, specifically with a crowbar, first.

Braintree snorted, then laughed softly as he shook his head. "You got me, Sis. When 'Brad Penney' turned up in town, I figured it was no accident. Not after Andre Thibodeaux was taken out by a hit-and-run driver as soon as he got out of prison. It was either the newsie or me, and it wasn't gonna be me. I'd just had breakfast at the City Café and I saw Hirsch—Penney—going into the shipping entrance at the Biersal. I followed him. When I saw he was in there alone, I grabbed a crowbar off the rack of tools. You can fill in the rest."

"Why didn't you try to talk to him, see what he was really planning to do?"

Braintree shook his head. "It was an accident. I was running from the cops. I didn't see the lady and the kid until it was too late. You know what safety glass looks like when it breaks? It's like a spider web, and the light catches on every little line. Real hard to drive with your windshield like that. I slid off the road into the ditch and the troopers fished me out. They knew what happened. The feds told me if I gave up Thibodeaux, I wouldn't be charged with the hit-and-run. Wouldn't be charged with a single blessed thing."

"Well, clearly you've reevaluated your life and changed your ways."

"Business is business, Sis. But now I've got a problem. I like you—I do. It's nothing personal, okay? But now you know some stuff that's gonna be a problem for me. And a businessman has to solve problems if he wants to stay in business."

PC looked toward the bar. Joaquin was nowhere to be seen.

"What? You gonna take me out back and shoot me?"

"Unfortunately, you are going to be filled with despair and take your own life by jumping off the roof of the motel."

"That dog won't hunt. Nobody'll believe it."

Braintree stood up, and PC wasn't too surprised to see a gun in his hand. He reached out and pulled her pendant towards himself, studying it. "You probably aren't aware, but I conduct a lot of confidential business here. The bar's equipped with signal jammers, just in case anybody's listening in. Nobody likes a rat, after all. Now, let's go."

Where's Harry Houdini when you need him? How am I going to get out of this?

He took PC's arm and jerked her roughly up. "We'll take the back elevator."

"Well, isn't that handy." PC muttered.

They cut through the laundry room to the freight elevator used by the cleaning and maintenance staff. The walls were covered in stained grey mover's quilts that covered the handrails. A blotch on the floor looked suspiciously like old blood, and PC wondered who else had taken a ride in this elevator. Her mind cast about frantically, looking for an escape.

What was it Mike always said? *Improvise. Adapt. Overcome. Anything can be a weapon if you can figure out how to use it.*

What did she have on her? Her FlitBit fitness tracker, the pendant with the hidden microphone, which might be working now that they were away from the jamming equipment. Shoes. Shoelaces. She'd left her bag in Tran's car, so no cell phone, pen, or keys.

The elevator door opened into a noisy mechanical room, with another door opposite the elevator. Braintree pushed the door and led her to a long, flat section of the roof, populated with HVAC equipment. On the far edge was a satellite dish with a coil of cable next to it.

The motel was only three stories. If she was able to find something below to break her fall, she might survive this. But Braintree would see the same things she could, and she doubted he'd let her pick the jumping off point.

You need a diversion so you can get the gun. That voice in her head sounded more like Mike's than her own.

Her wrist itched, and her fingers fell on her FlitBit. *There's a timer with an alarm.*

She surreptitiously set it for two seconds. *One one hundred. Two one hundred. Three one hundred?*

The watch buzzed and beeped, startling Braintree. PC lunged for his gun hand, clamping her teeth on his wrist with everything she had. He yelped and she heard metal clatter on the concrete roof.

She dove for the gun. The kick Braintree aimed at her ribs glanced off her hip, knocking her off balance. Pain seared her shoulder as she collided with the hard grille of a condenser unit, but she caught the gun before it skittered under the equipment. PC was vaguely aware of a rhythmic, metallic clunking noise behind her as she grabbed the weapon and rolled over, pointing it at Braintree.

He laughed. A loud belly laugh. Not the reaction PC typically got on those rare occasions when she had needed to point a gun at somebody.

The detective looked down. Something was wrong with the gun. The grip didn't feel right in her hand. Too deep. Too chunky. She glanced at it and noticed a glowing green bar at the top of the grip.

Dammit.

A smart gun, keyed to Braintree's biometrics. It was useless to her.

Throw it! Throw it! Don't let him get it.

She tossed the hunk of metal as hard as she could. But the HVAC equipment was in the way, so she wasn't able to heave it as far as she'd have liked. Still, it was on the sloping part of the roof, and it would be difficult for Braintree to get at it.

He growled and started toward her.

Get to the satellite. Move!

She scrambled toward the dish.

Now what?

Breeze made the loose cable between the bowl and the coil sway.

Jump! Now!

PC grabbed the cable and flung herself off the roof. She wished she'd been wearing gloves, because she felt her skin blistering from the friction as the plastic snaked through her hands.

The jolt when the cable ran out almost knocked her right off her lifeline. Her palms felt like they were on fire. She couldn't hold on any longer. She let go and dropped about eight feet into a weed-filled flowerbed.

Above her, she heard Tran shout, "Don't move! Hands in the air where I can see them."

PC sat on the chipped concrete bench in front of the *Best Southern Motel*. When Woody had led a handcuffed Braintree past her, he'd grinned. "Oh, Sis. I thought we were friends." He chuckled to himself all the way to the parking lot.

The paramedics had just left after giving her a once-over and bandaging her raw, blistered hands. Not much to be done about the bruised shoulder.

Tran sat next to her. "You okay?"

"Not sure. Ask me tomorrow."

"You know, we were about to go in after you when your wire went dead. Joaquin came out and told us Braintree was taking you up to the roof. Chief and I climbed up the fire escape. And let me tell you, that thing was so rusty, I was sure it was going to crumble to pieces with every step. Gorman and Sanchez watched the entrances. I almost had a heart attack when I saw you plummet over the side of the building."

"Little adrenalin now and then's good for you."

He laughed. "Maybe. We didn't get the confession for Penney's murder on tape, but thanks to you, we had probable cause to search his office. It's a treasure trove of stolen goods."

It was PC's turn to laugh. "Really? Did you find Simone's quilts or Daphne Jones' socks?"

He shook his head. "No trace of them yet."

A puff of wind ruffled PC's hair and skimmed down her back. She got to her feet, her muscles a little stiffer than she expected. "You're giving me a ride back to my car, right?"

Chapter 16

PC LEANED AGAINST the wooden fence and looked up at the stars. She scratched Guinevere's head, despite her throbbing hands. Cordite trotted around the yard behind her, snuffling at what was probably 'possum spoor. She was still jittery from almost having been thrown off the top of the *Best Southern Motel* by Hunter Braintree. She hadn't been able to eat dinner, and she was afraid to sleep, knowing nightmares waited in the dark behind her eyelids.

The stars glittered and twinkled against the black velvet of the night sky. Cold and distant, they still comforted her. She knew it wasn't true, but she still liked to think that Mike was one of those twinkling lights in the sky. Some of the deepest conversations they'd had were when they were far from the light pollution of the city, lying on the ground next to each other, looking for shooting stars or other astronomical events.

When she had been up on that roof, trying to figure out how to escape, it was almost like he had been standing beside her, whispering in her ear.

Was his death her fault, too?

If they hadn't been arguing about something stupid.

If he hadn't been angry when he left, he might have been more aware of his surroundings and not gotten hit by the drunk driver.

If she had driven a little faster to the hospital.

If. If. If.

Now she wondered if what Dinah Mae had said during the ghost tour was true. *If we never let go of our grief, we trap our loved ones here with us and never let them cross over to where they're supposed to go.*

She sniffled as a tear trickled down her cheek. PC had always scoffed at the idea of ghosts. If ghosts would only appear and tell her who killed them and why, that would have made her job a thousand times easier. But it had never happened. The faces of the murder victims that haunted her dreams weren't so much ghosts as indelible images seared into her brain, branded there by the worst humanity had to offer.

But the feeling that Mike was there with her, whispering in her ear, was so real. She could swear she felt his breath on her cheek. The warm draft of air might just have come from the HVAC equipment on the roof, though.

Gwen raised her head and nibbled her lip along PC's wrist. A donkey caress.

In October, the Earth passes through the debris field of Halley's comet, resulting in the Orionid meteor showers, and PC had been hoping to see some streaking across the sky. Nothing yet—perhaps the moon was too bright. It was on its way toward the horizon, though, so there was still a chance.

She took in a deep breath and let it out slowly. *Maybe this is dumb. Dead is dead and you are probably just in my imagination. But if you can hear me, Mike, I'm sorry. Sorry I picked a fight with you over the stupid catering menu. Sorry I didn't make it to the hospital. Sorry if I have been holding on to you so tight you can't move on to your next adventure. I have never stopped loving you. Thank you for saving my life this evening. But if you need to move on... I don't know what to say. I release you? Fly free? Godspeed? I don't know. Just be at peace.*

Gwen's head suddenly twisted away and PC followed her gaze. A magnesium white meteor with a long blue tail arced across the infinite sky. Most shooting stars flared and burned out quickly—a blink at the wrong time would miss them. But this one stayed for a few seconds before it faded.

Was that a sign, or just a standard Orionid? Guess it's whatever I decide it is.

She gave Guinevere a final scratch, called Cordite, and they headed inside.

Terry preferred not to drive at night, so PC drove him and Rose to the Halloween Ball at the Afters. Her hands had mostly healed, but the new skin was still tender. She wore evening gloves to protect them, but they felt weird on her forearms.

Drew would meet them there. The small lot was already full, and the Biersal next door allowed overflow parking, so PC dropped her mother and Terry off at the entrance. She caught a glimpse of Drew standing on the back verandah, waiting for them to arrive. She couldn't help but smile at how handsome he looked in his tux and black tie.

Terry gestured toward PC's SUV, and Drew hurried down the steps toward her. She rolled down the window to speak with him, but he pulled open the door and got inside.

"Can't stand around twiddling my thumbs while you walk back alone."

PC snorted. "It's just across the street."

She shifted into drive and they went in search of a parking spot. Most of the Biersal's lot was also occupied, but they did find a slot next to a light pole. PC stepped out of the car into the pool of mercury vapor light.

Drew stared at her over the hood. "You look... stunning."

The detective was suddenly self-conscious. The vee neckline of the lacey bodice plunged deeper than she was really comfortable with. But then again, she should have known better than to have taken Daisy shopping with her.

"Thanks. You look great, too."

He held out his elbow, and she pulled up her shimmery skirt high enough to avoid tripping over road hazards before taking his arm. They promenaded together to the Afters and stepped into the front parlor. An animatronic werewolf greeted them with a low growl and glowing eyes. They moved through to the ballroom.

PC gaped at the decorations. A giant, furry spider lurked in one corner, and ropy cobwebs dangled from the ceiling around it. Mechanical bats fluttered above the guests' heads on a track. A skeleton butler offered a tray of canapes. Stuffed sheet ghosts floated along the walls, no doubt held up by fishing line. Brightly painted sugar skulls decorated the serving tables.

"Let's get some punch," Drew said, pulling her out of her wonderment.

Rose and Terry stood near the crystal punch bowl, chatting with Jim and Winnie Hargraves. PC said hello before reaching for the punch ladle. She dropped it as a plastic eyeball popped up and rolled lazily in the red liquid. It gave her the heebie-jeebies, reminding her of a particularly gruesome case she'd worked on.

She found a bottle of water instead. The rest of the refreshments were much tamer—black cat and jack-o'-lantern cookies, witch rice crispy treats, and green breadsticks with a sliced almond 'fingernail.' She might get something later.

A woman in voluminous skirts passed by. Not so large as a crinoline, but more than one tulle petticoat. The back of the dress was open to just below her waist, and the whole thing glittered with sequins. A bejeweled fascinator dominated her elaborate up-do.

PC turned to her mother. "Was that Renetta Sherman?"

"Yes. She's been struttin' around like the cock of the walk the last two days. Seems she was able to win the bid for the *Best South-*

ern Motel. Thorne Marberger's helpin' her out—would you believe that? They're gonna knock the place down and put up a Possum-wood-themed hotel. Decoratin' will be done usin' stuff from local artists. Brew from the Biersal will be on tap. They plan to set up delivery from all the local restaurants instead of room service. They want mobile groomin' from the vet's office, too, for people travelin' with their dogs."

"That sounds like an ambitious project," Drew said. "Renetta had called and said she wanted to come to the gallery and talk to me but didn't give specifics."

"Well, Thorne Marberger's got more money than God, so if he wants it to work, it will. With that new tollway comin' in, I'm sure they'll make money hand over fist." Winnie took a bite of sugar cookie black cat.

Jim Hargraves waved a breadstick. "You are still going to be around for the tree lighting ceremony next month, right PC? It's the Saturday after Thanksgiving—you can get a jump on your holiday shopping. It's a whole day festival. There's an arts and crafts fair and food vendors during the day, then when it gets dark, they have the high school choir come and sing some Christmas songs. Phineas Scott plugs in the tree and everybody stands around *oohing* and *ahhing*.

PC felt five sets of eyeballs on her.

Drew's hand brushed hers.

"Sure. I wouldn't miss it."

If you enjoyed this book, please consider leaving a review at your favorite book site. Reviews help other readers find and enjoy new books!

Other books by Holly Dey:

Manor of Death: The Possumwood Mysteries Book 1

Death on the Half Shell: The Possumwood Mysteries Book 2

Azalea Trail of Death: The Possumwood Mysteries Book 3

Death Re-Enacted: The Possumwood Mysteries Book 4

Death Rides a Bobcat: The Possumwood Mysteries Book 5

Key to Death: The Possumwood Mysteries Book 6

Death Curated: The Possumwood Mysteries Book 7

Pool of Death: The Possumwood Mysteries Book 8

All Death No Cattle: The Possumwood Mysteries Book 9

Death is Lager than Life: The Possumwood Mysteries Book 10

Art of Death: The Possumwood Mysteries Book 11

Little Town of Death-Lehem: The Possumwood Mysteries Book 12

Winter: Boxset Collection Books 1-3

Spring: Boxset Collection Books 4-6

Summer: Boxset Collection Books 7-9

Fall: Boxset Collection Books 10-12

Large Print Editions

Manor of Death: The Possumwood Mysteries Large Print Edition Book 1

Death on the Half Shell: The Possumwood Mysteries Large Print Edition Book 2

Azalea Trail of Death: The Possumwood Mysteries Large Print Edition Book 3

Death Re-Enacted: The Possumwood Mysteries Large Print Edition Book 4

Death Rides a Bobcat: The Possumwood Mysteries Large Print Edition Book 5

Key to Death: The Possumwood Mysteries Large Print Edition Book 6

Death Curated: The Possumwood Mysteries Large Print Edition Book 7

Pool of Death: The Possumwood Mysteries Large Print Edition Book 8

All Death No Cattle: The Possumwood Mysteries Large Print Edition Book 9

Death is Lager than Life: The Possumwood Mysteries Large Print Edition Book 10

Art of Death: The Possumwood Mysteries Large Print Edition Book 11

Little Town of Death-Lehem: The Possumwood Mysteries Large Print Edition Book 12

www.ingramcontent.com/pod-product-compliance
Lightning Source LLC
Chambersburg PA
CBHW061252170626
46809CB00007B/2953